PRAISE FOR ANELA'S CLUB

"Anela's inspiring journey is a testimony to how we all can rise from traumatic darkness to brilliant change and growth."

—**Joanne P. McCallie,** Six-Time NCAA Women's Basketball Coach of the Year, Duke University, Author of *Secret Warrior*

"Touching, moving, human—and profoundly intelligent."

—**J. Mark Ramseyer,** Mitsubishi Professor of Japanese Legal Studies, Harvard University, Author of *Contracting in Japan*

"*Anela's Club*, at first, reads like playing checkers, but this is nothing less than a chess game on life. Enlightening . . . and strong."

—**Dino Babers,** ACC Football Coach of the Year, Syracuse University

"Aimed at teen readers but perfect for the teen still living in all of us. The final scenes are emotional, and I admit it, tear-worthy."

—**David Patneaude,** Award-Winning Young Adult Fiction Author, including *Thin Wood Walls*

"A poetic story and powerfully told, showing us that deep childhood trauma has the ability to break or make us, and the happenstance of a mentor with the right words."

—**Dianne C. Braley**, Author of *The Silence and the Sound*, NYC 2022 Big Book Award Winner

"D. K. Yamashiro is arguably the world's leading expert on the childhood trauma experienced by U.S. presidents. In *Anela's Club*, he provides a masterful story that can help people through personal trauma."

—**Gary Scott Smith**, PhD, Author of *Faith and the Presidency* and *Religion in the Oval Office*

"I loved every part of *Anela's Club*, as I read it in one sitting. There are lessons in Anela's story for all of us to learn from."

—**Bill Sheehan**, Author of *A Tail Among Tales*

"*Anela's Club* is a triumph! Whether we are dealing with trauma or not, we all need to become ourselves. It lifts the heart to be a part of Anela's Club."

—**Eleanor M. Cooper**, EdD, Author of *Dragonfly Dreams*, Benjamin Franklin Award Winner

"I loved meeting D. K. Yamashiro's Anela and joining her club. Highly recommended."

—**Lynn Seldon**, Author of *Carolina's Ring*

"I most appreciated the clear message of being true to oneself in the face of peer pressure; and finding and holding onto hope, even in what can be some very dark hours in our lives."

—**Anne E. C. McCants**, PhD, Ann F. Friedlaender Professor of History at MIT

"This story of a resilient young woman will inspire any reader. Yamashiro guides us through Anela's dreams and challenges, and gives us, too, her great blessing: hope."

—**William R. Cross**, Chair of the Advisory Board, Yale Center for Faith and Culture, Author of *Winslow Homer: American Passage*

"Anela's determination shines brightly, connecting us with the human side of politics. Love and hope are tested in this wonderful page turner."

—**Kathleen Reid**, Author of *Secrets in the Palazzo*, Pencraft Award Winner 2022

"Thought-provoking and timeless... offering touch points for diverse audiences, particularly youth navigating the complex terrain of tragedy, abandonment, and self-doubt."

—**Hugh H. Dunn**, PhD, Director of the Pacific Literacy Consortium, University of Hawaii, Author of *Kahai's Journey*

"An impressive, inspiring read for adolescents and adults alike. As a former teacher, I think high school kids really need to read this . . ."

—**Maia Evrigenis,** Author of *Neon Jane*

"I couldn't put *Anela's Club* down . . . I would urge any person at every age who has felt inadequate to devour this book. It is food for the soul. D. K. Yamashiro has created and polished a tour de force!"

—**Doug Bond,** PhD, Lecturer in Extension, Harvard University

"A poignant story featuring a powerful refrain of despair, resilience, and hope."

—**Mia Chung,** Concert Pianist, Music Professor, Executive Director, Octet Collaborative at MIT

"D. K. Yamashiro does an exceptional job of showing how one can overcome adversity through the support of those that love and care for them, even in the most unlikely of people."

—**Duane Coleman,** EdD, Former Superintendent of Schools, Oceanside Unified School District

"A powerful story of resilience and grit. Against so many odds, Anela chooses to grow and learn from her circumstances, change her mindset, and persevere to change her future."

—**Emily Burdett,** DPhil, Assistant Professor, School of Psychology, University of Nottingham

Anela's Club

by D. K. Yamashiro

© Copyright 2024 D. K. Yamashiro

ISBN 979-8-88824-222-3

All rights reserved. No part of this publication may be reproduced, stored in a retrieval system, or transmitted in any form or by any means—electronic, mechanical, photocopy, recording, or any other—except for brief quotations in printed reviews, without the prior written permission of the author.

This is a work of fiction. All the characters in this book are fictitious, and any resemblance to actual persons, living or dead, is purely coincidental. The names, incidents, dialogue, and opinions expressed are products of the author's imagination and are not to be construed as real.

Published by

köehlerbooks™

3705 Shore Drive
Virginia Beach, VA 23455
800-435-4811
www.koehlerbooks.com

ANELA'S CLUB

A NOVEL

ANELA'S CLUB

A NOVEL

D.K. YAMASHIRO

VIRGINIA BEACH
CAPE CHARLES

To
Jamie
Allie, Hugh, and Luke
SDG

CHAPTER 1

Today marked the first time in two months I woke up without that hollow feeling clawing at my insides, robbing me of decent sleep. Sure, I woke with a start. It could have been the rap music blasting from the car driving past my window or the morning noise from the neighbors bleeding through the walls. All I know is that for the first time in quite a while, I felt anticipation. There was something big out there, waiting for me. What it was, I didn't know. But I could feel it.

Two months ago, my brother, Jake, died. I'd lost count of how many times I wished it was me instead. I mourned my brother's death and the past we shared—but more than that, and worse, the future we would never have.

Jake had so much more to give the world than I did. He was my protector, my rock. And then he was gone. Today, after months of relentless silence, I allowed myself to remember.

Two months ago, I'd just thrown my hat in the ring for class president, which meant giving a stirring speech to inspire the kids to vote for me. Writing it was the easy part. Getting up in front of everyone and presenting the speech was the big roadblock in my path.

"So, which is it, Anela?" Jake asked. "Is this the springboard for a remarkable young woman fighting her way to the top? Or a case of fear and doubt chipping away at her until there's nothing left to fight with?"

"What if I make a fool of myself?" I said.

Jake adopted the outraged expression he reserved for my moments of doubt. It usually made me laugh. "What if the sky was purple and money grew on trees?" he said. "Let me tell you what happens if you make a fool of yourself. You climb on top of the foolishness and grow taller. Do you hear me?"

That was my daily affirmation: Jake telling me I could be whatever I wanted to be. I was the queen of insecurity, ruling a land of indecision. Self-doubt circled like a hungry shark. I didn't become class president, but I got through the speech and received solid applause.

Jake told me again and again that nothing was out of my reach. I simply had to figure out what I wanted to contribute to the world. He said I should be patient, and one day it would just come to me. But how would I know when it arrived?

"It's a warm feeling in the pit of your stomach," he said, "that spreads to your head and ends up in your heart. You just know."

"You mean the way you feel about football?"

Jake became quiet, as if looking inside himself and not liking what he saw there. He shrugged, then put on a smile. "Football is all right."

Jake was seventeen, a year and a half older than I was. Unlike me, Jake seemed to have found his purpose in the world. He fell into that 1 percent of people born with a gift, his future in professional football all but guaranteed.

I was shocked the day I realized that Jake wasn't living his dream by playing football. Instead, he was living our parents' dream. He was their pride and joy, their reason to soldier on as our family unraveled. Maybe that was why Jake kept coaching me to be the best I could be. My parents didn't expect much, if anything, from me. Unlike Jake, I was free to do what I wanted with my life.

As to our family falling apart, Mom's patience had worn down to a thread, and Dad was usually pickled and in no mood to put up with her aggravation. The tension usually started building around early evening, with their anger at each other growing into this towering roller coaster of threats and accusations. Jake shrugged it off, but I knew it stressed him out just as much as it did me.

Most evenings, he and I hung out at the library until we figured things had cooled down, or until they closed. Jake picked the library because he knew I loved reading—and because of the pretty girl who worked there as assistant librarian.

"You should ask her out," I suggested more than once.

"One day."

Maybe Jake was shy, or insecure about approaching a girl older than him. We didn't discuss it after that, and since he never asked for advice, I didn't push it. Contrary to the advice he gave me, I suppose Jake dealt with his own insecurities by ignoring them. He had to tough it out when he was bullied as a junior. One boy called him "Chink" all the time. Jake took the abuse for a month, then challenged the bully to a fight. It was brutal, bloody, and lasted all of three minutes. Jake walked away the champ.

Stories of the fight spread like wildfire. Since Jake always took a firm stance against violence, I called him out on the hypocrisy. He shrugged and said fighting was his last resort because rationally debating the bully didn't work. A few days after the fight, the bully's father came to school and watched his son apologize to Jake. And Jake, being the person he was, accepted the apology and said that as far as he was concerned, they could start with a clean slate.

Jake's skin color, like mine, was walnut brown, though more beach sand was mixed into his. He took after our Italian mother, with her Roman nose and light skin and my father's Asian eyes. Me, I took after our father, with his dark Hawaiian skin and frizzy Polynesian hair that refused to be tamed no matter how hard I worked the wild curls. I once tried to straighten my hair the way I'd seen some Black girls at school do it, but I ended up with some parts of my hair straight and others a frizzy mess. I had to wear a cap for weeks to cover it up. After that, I gave up trying to follow trends, deciding my time was better spent on schoolwork.

The main thing Jake got from Dad was his size—that and his talent for throwing a football and dodging tackles. The sad thing is, if Jake hadn't been able to do that, he'd still be alive. The irony of that left a void so big and empty I couldn't breathe. The hungry shark closed in and swallowed me whole as what little support I had vanished. I was lost.

Mom had no comfort to give. She clung to her own grief and built an even higher wall between us. Dad became more of a stranger, and his drinking got a hundred times worse. He was drowning his anguish and killing himself in the process. Whatever my parents had left to say to each other was communicated with shouts and irritation. More than once, neighbors hammered on the walls to shut them up. There was no bringing this family together in its time of mourning.

At times, I took flight, walking the streets aimlessly to give them time to calm down. We didn't live in the safest neighborhood, but my desperation to escape Mom and Dad trumped security concerns.

One night, as I walked past the Dollar Store, a few rough-looking guys hollered at me. My pulse went into overdrive. When I picked up the pace, one of the guys stepped in front of me.

"'Sup, baby girl?" he said with an ugly grin. "Where you goin'?"

I tried to sidestep him, but he was too slick. He forced me back until I was against the wall. I smelled the booze on his breath and recognized the drunk, reckless look glazing his eyes. The few people nearby ignored us. A chill ran down my back when the guy's hand touched my cheek and forced my chin up so I had to meet his glare.

"I don't like gettin' shut down when all I'm doin' is tryin' to be friendly," he hissed. "So what do you say we start over?"

A big guy plucked him away from me. "That's Jake's li'l sister, fool."

Suddenly free, I ran away as fast as I could. I didn't look back until I reached my apartment block. No one followed me. I was safe. Even in death, Jake was protecting me.

So, this was my choice: escape Mom and Dad's vicious fights and face danger on the streets, or stay inside while they tore my soul to shreds.

A week after the funeral, my parents split up. Neither bothered to sit me down and explain things. It was like I didn't exist. I knew Jake was their world, but I never realized their world didn't include even the smallest piece of me. The night Dad left, I came home to a silent apartment. He took the TV and his favorite chair. Since he had no money for a place of his own, I suspected he moved into Grandma's basement.

That evening, I watched as Mom made food to take to her night job.

"Where did he go?" I asked.

She shrugged. "Don't know. Don't care."

"Is he coming back?" I don't know why I asked. The answer was written in the wrinkles of our family history.

"No," she said. "I doubt he'll bother us again. Now he can drink himself to death in peace."

Dad never called me or left a message to say goodbye. Maybe I was last on his list of priorities. Who knew what went on in his head? If he wanted to talk to me, he'd find a way. I wasn't sure why I cared; I couldn't remember having a conversation with him. Dad's sphere was limited to football, Jake, and booze.

That was the end of our fragile little family. The sudden silence in the apartment was crushing. The walls seemed to close in on me. All I could do was run outside and shut the door on my angst. Or try to.

I walked around the neighborhood for miles while it was still daylight. Expending all that energy made me hungry, and all I had to fill the gap in my stomach were the ramen noodle packs Mom bought in bulk at the Dollar Store. Jake and I used to buy our own food, usually fixings for hearty sandwiches. We'd sit at the small kitchen table and have long conversations until Mom or Dad came home.

Sometimes we got lucky, and there'd be no commotion, Mom and Dad being too tired to fight. If the screaming started, Jake would put our sandwiches in small brown bags, and we'd eat on the bus on the way to the library. After Jake's death, it was ramen noodles or nothing. The apartment was finally quiet, but there was no peace in my heart, and I didn't feel like eating. Something inside me still expected a fight outside the bedroom door.

At school, my grades slipped. I grew detached. Boston's confusingly named Brooklyn High School didn't like students slacking off. Even the kids frowned upon it, like it was a stain on their prestige. Every kid had to excel at something and give it their all.

An award-winning public school with both a ton of rich folks in its district and a lot of low-income households, Brooklyn High prided itself on being the United Nations of schools and embracing everyone.

Except slackers.

CHAPTER 2

After months of me sulking and feeling sorry for myself, the sympathy of students and teachers had run dry, and I was close to suspension, waiting for the axe to fall. It wasn't like I had a family that would notice. With Jake gone, no one cared—except my social studies teacher, Miss DeGracia.

The day before I awoke with renewed optimism, she decided to pull out all the stops and have a heart-to-heart with me in the hall before classes.

"I see you didn't sign up for the class trip tomorrow," she said.

Miss DeGracia was a perfect blend of confidence and grace. She had long black hair worn in a ponytail, and I felt like her big brown eyes could gaze right into my soul. The last thing I wanted was to disappoint her.

"If it's the forty-dollar fee," she said, "we can make a plan."

The school had a special fund for "less privileged" kids: money for school lunches and other expenses. Rebellion rose in my chest.

"I'm not a charity case," I said. "Maybe I just don't want to go."

I regretted the words before they ran cold. Because if anyone was on my side, it was Miss DeGracia. I didn't know how to say I was sorry, so I just stood there, casting moody looks at the ground. As much as I wanted the wall I'd built to crumble, it stood strong.

"See, I thought you would appreciate this trip more than anyone," Miss DeGracia said evenly. "I guess I was wrong. We'll miss you. Maybe next time."

I thought I'd been dismissed, but she wasn't about to give up.

"At least tell me why you don't want to come," she insisted. "Be honest. You should know by now this is a judgment-free zone."

Of course I wanted to go on the trip. The class was going to the State House to see a live senate session, and social studies was my favorite subject. I kept an A there even when my other grades were falling.

"Like you said, maybe next time," I mumbled. I wasn't going to admit it was about the money. We could barely make rent, let alone pay for class trips. And I refused to apply for help from the fund. I guess pride overran good sense.

Miss DeGracia locked eyes with me. Uncomfortable silence stretched out for an eternity. I started looking for an escape.

"Let me know if anything changes," Miss DeGracia said. "Also, I'll be assigning all my classes a five-hundred-word essay that will count toward the final grade."

The way she said it—casual but loaded with innuendo—rattled me. Did she know about my side hustle? Was this a trap? Or a hint?

In the months before his death, Jake helped me run a little business to earn some cash. Some of the rich-kid athletes didn't care about academics, but they had to keep up their grades to stay on the school teams. Since I was all about social studies and history, Jake spread the word to his less academically inclined pals that I could do their essays for forty dollars per five hundred words.

Not too bad since one essay only took me an hour, if that. And I loved writing them. Jake conducted business arrangements during lunch in the cafeteria. If you didn't get your name on the list and hand Jake the full amount in cash, you were out of luck. I tried to give him a commission, but he wouldn't have it. He had his own side gig as a personal trainer to some of these same kids.

In any given week, I was making two hundred bucks easy. It got to the point where I was nervous about keeping the cash at home. I needed a bank account. So I took a bus to the bank, hands clutching my backpack with a stack of cash inside, my heart beating in my throat all the way—first because I might get robbed, but also because I expected pushback at the bank, me being Anela from the hood. But the lady was nice as could be. I introduced myself and said I needed to open a bank account.

"How old are you, Anela?" she asked.

"I'm fifteen years and five months," I said, confused. What did age have to do with putting money in a bank?

"You have to be eighteen years old if you want to open an account," the lady said. "Otherwise, you need a parent or legal guardian to cosign."

How could I explain that getting one of my parents to cosign would open a can of worms that didn't need to be opened?

"So why don't you ask your mom or dad to come in with you next time, and we'll take care of the paperwork then."

I nodded, my mind already exploring other possibilities. Jake would know what to do.

"Okay, thanks for your help," I said as politely as possible. "I'll get one of my parents to come with me." That was a lie. I was saving up for college, and that was a secret best kept between Jake and me.

I couldn't believe I had to make the trip back home with all that cash on me. I felt like everyone knew about the six thousand dollars I was hiding in my backpack. I texted Jake and explained my dilemma. He texted back a row of laughing emojis and said he had a plan.

That night, he showed me the small, homemade "vault" he had created under one of the grungy floorboards in his room. I saw some money rolled up in neat little bundles. There was also a gun. I must have flinched, because the next thing I felt was Jake's hand on my arm.

"Easy there, sis."

"What are you doing with a gun?" I whispered, my insides churning at the sight of it.

"To protect us," Jake whispered back.

"Protect us from what?"

"You can live in this neighborhood, in this house, and ask me that?"

"Where did you get it?"

"Anela, stop. You're acting like I'm a fool. I know what I'm doing, all right?"

"Okay, I'm sorry," I said. "I'm just a little shocked. Give me a break."

"You can't tell anyone, though."

"Who am I going to tell, Jake? That's so stupid."

"I can show you how to use it."

"Thank you, but no thank you. I don't like guns."

"Neither do I," Jake said finally. "But it's better to have one and not need it than need one and not have it."

Jake was sensible, and I trusted him.

"Fine, show me," I said.

He didn't show off. He took the gun out and went through a few basic steps so I knew how to use it. He had me hold it, feel its weight. It fit in the palm of my hand but wielded the power of life and death. I was scared and awed at the same time and quickly handed the gun back, burying Jake's instructions in the back of my mind. It wasn't like I'd ever need them. But like he said, it was a necessary evil.

I rolled my money into bundles like Jake did with his. I had a velvet pouch covered with glitter that I got from Tamara for Christmas one year, back when we were still friends. My fat money rolls filled the pouch, and Jake tucked it inside the vault. Knowing my money was safe felt good. The gun still made me nervous, though. To me, there was no worse sound than a gun going off. But Jake seemed to have a good grip on the pros and cons of owning one, and I got more relaxed about it as time went by.

Sometimes, when things got tight, I'd sneak a few hundred bucks to my mom. She never asked where I got the money. Maybe she was afraid of the answer. We didn't talk a lot, so there was never a moment to slip in that I got paid for helping rich kids write essays for social studies. Besides, she would have found something to criticize.

I filled up another glitter pouch after that, but Jake's funeral expenses took it all, and his money too. I could have let the county cremate him and give us Jake's ashes in a plain box, but I cringed at the thought. My parents didn't have cash for a proper funeral, so I paid. After that, the only thing left in Jake's vault was the gun.

The funeral director was kind and gave me a break. The service was more elaborate than what I paid for. I just wanted Jake to have the funeral he deserved. I stopped writing essays after that. Jake had handled the "business side," and my self-confidence was in the sewer. Which was why I didn't have the measly forty bucks for the class trip.

Miss DeGracia sighed. "Anela, I know my students. And I know the athletes are not here to major in social studies. They just want to pass their grade and move on."

"You knew about the essays all this time?" I asked. "Never mind. Don't answer that."

I tried to get a grip on my mixed feelings. *Should I say thank you for not telling? Does she want a cut? What is the deal here?* I felt like I was on a precipice.

Miss DeGracia smiled. She'd said what she wanted to say. It was up to me to figure out what she meant. That I could start it up again, maybe? I took a leap.

"I don't think I can do it by myself," I said. "Jake was the mastermind."

"Listen to me. You can do anything you want. I know you're going through a tough time, and things might get even tougher before they get better. But the number-one starting point is not questioning your abilities."

I knew she was trying to get me psyched. She reminded me of Jake that way. How did I explain to her that an invisible harness was holding me back? Any plans I cooked up were stymied by that little voice inside that said I wasn't good enough to succeed.

"How many people from my neighborhood manage to go to college?" I said.

Miss DeGracia rolled her eyes and shook her head, exasperated. "You're looking at one," she said. "My parents came here when I was a baby. Even with both working two jobs, there was no money for college. But they made sure I worked hard in my classes, and in my last year of high school, I won a scholarship."

"You can win a scholarship?" I asked, intrigued. "I didn't know you could win one if you didn't play a sport."

"Of course," Miss DeGracia said. "If you want to go to college, there are a lot of avenues. Let me ask you a question. Do you have an idea what you want to do with your future?"

"Not really. Well, not yet."

"Figure that out. Then we can talk about your options. You need to open yourself up to all the possibilities. Looking for excuses only closes doors."

"Okay, that's fair, but—"

"Stop with the 'buts,' Anela." She went to her desk and handed me a pink book. The cover featured a gentle-looking girl in a hijab. The title was *I Am Malala*. "Do you know the story of Malala Yousafzai?"

"Isn't that the girl who was shot on her way to school?"

"Yes, but she's more than that. The Taliban tried to silence her, but she stood up to them. She survived the attack on her life and went on to win the Nobel Peace Prize. This is her autobiography."

"That's pretty cool."

"You should get to class. We'll continue this discussion another time."

"Okay, thanks for the book," I said, thinking we were done.

But Miss DeGracia had one more thing to add. "You're so incredibly smart, Anela. All it's going to take is for you to realize that."

Tears suddenly filled my eyes and clung to my cheeks. Someone showing genuine concern for me felt a little overwhelming. I hadn't experienced that since Jake died. I nodded and dashed down the hall.

I made my way to English class in a daze. With Jake to push me, I sometimes had a handle on my insecurities. These days, not so much. If I was so smart, why couldn't I get rid of the countless things holding me back? Why couldn't I accept my parents' neglect as their problem and not mine? Instead, I was always looking at myself, trying to figure out what was wrong with me that made them not care. I could never figure it out, though, and the chasm between us grew wider, until there wasn't a bridge long enough to cross it.

CHAPTER 3

Back when my essay fund was still growing, Jake and I went to the computer store so I could buy a laptop. It took hours and many questions before we settled on one. Jake helped me set up Wi-Fi because my phone had a data limit. Suddenly, I could write twice as many essays, and business boomed.

One night, my mom came into my room without knocking. There was no time to hide the new laptop. Her gaze stuck to the shiny lid, and for a moment, I thought she might go into a rage.

"Where'd you get that?" she asked. "You didn't steal it, did you?"

I shook my head so hard I thought I'd kink my neck. "No. Why would you even ask that? I bought it with money I saved."

Again, she didn't ask where the money for my "savings" came from. But if she thought I might steal a laptop, I shuddered to think what else she might be thinking. She stood in the doorway for a while, like she had something to say but no way to say it. I smiled like an idiot, trying to bridge the discomfort between us. Finally, she blinked.

"What do you need it for?"

"Schoolwork, research. Everything is done on computers these days."

"Instead of playing on that thing, you could get a part-time job. Help pay the bills."

"This is working toward my future."

"It's that fancy school stuffing your head with ideas. Pay attention to how the real world works, Anela. Dreaming gets you nowhere."

After that, I gave her more money every week to help pay the bills—literally trying to buy her love, but of course it didn't work. And I ran out of money after Jake died anyway.

My parents poured all their energy into Jake's future in football, and Mom had the additional burden of keeping Dad from drinking himself to death. I was pretty much an afterthought—as if my fate was sealed the day I was born.

We never had the little heart-to-hearts moms and daughters are supposed to have. I learned about my period at school. Poor Jake had to explain the workings of womanhood to me, and he stuttered and blushed through the main points. He left it up to me to find the more subtle details online. One afternoon, I found a small heating pad in a box on my bed. Jake and I never talked about it again, but he respected my space during a certain time of the month.

Anyway, all through English class—which was tamer than usual, but more on that later—I was thinking about Miss DeGracia's pep talk. There was no denying that my spirits got a boost. So, come lunchtime, I strolled into the cafeteria and all but announced to those who cared that I was back in the business of writing essays for cash.

The last two months, I'd just grab a sandwich and make myself scarce, not socializing. Now I stood in line, looking to pick up where I'd left off food-wise, too. I'd never been one to push my fork aimlessly around my plate. I planned on getting a full course of meatloaf and mashed potatoes since this would have to double for dinner. Now that it was just Mom and me and no extra money, I was a footnote to her existence. At home, it was Ramen City.

Of course, after a few minutes in the cafeteria, I started to doubt my ability to run the essay thing myself. I lacked Jake's coolness, his easygoing confidence. And all of my biggest "clients" were his pals. I'd cut many ties with my antisocial behavior, protesting life and any reason to live it. By cutting ties, I mean snipping them with a sharp pair of scissors. Trying to be strong and "move forward" was exhausting, so I eventually figured being alone was easier than coddling fake friendships. The few girls I hung around with cooled toward me after Jake's death. I realized too late that I had only been on their radar because of him. He was the good-looking football star with full-ride scholarships all lined up, and everyone knew that if they were nice to Jake's sister, he'd be nice to them.

For a few days after Jake's memorial, I got sympathetic glances and kids hugging me, some offering condolences. Two weeks later, I was invisible again. People don't dwell; it's human nature to move on, and I was okay with that, as long as they didn't expect me to do the same.

I peered around the cafeteria. It was weird to be back in the middle of a buzzing crowd. The lunch lady, Gloria, doubled up on the meatloaf, stacking my plate. She lived in my neighborhood and knew my mom. She leaned in and said, "We're doing a little salsa dancing Saturday night. You and your mom should come."

I smiled. "I'll tell her, but you know she won't."

"What's up with that? If I looked like her, I'd be dancing every Saturday night." Gloria shrugged and shook her head. At least she'd tried.

Gloria's daughter was my age and went to another school. She wasn't the academic type but had a YouTube channel where she discussed makeup and hair products and seemed to make good money, even if it wasn't the most sophisticated show in the world. I admired her entrepreneurship. She acknowledged her academic limitations and used what she was good at: telling other girls which affordable foundations and blushes sucked and which didn't.

I grabbed a fruit juice and looked for a place to sit. There were no pending invitations, and I was met with a bunch of blank stares, so I found a spot where I could eat in peace and be fairly visible to anyone down for essays for cash. My mounting doubts battled with my will to see how things played out. I reached into my backpack and pulled out *I Am Malala*.

"Hey, Anela!" someone yelled from a big table. I looked over to see rowdy boys peacocking and girls splashing on lip gloss and pushing salads around their plates. The group was known as the Bling Clique, and they were everything the name suggested. They ruled the fashion world at Brooklyn High, and their entire existence revolved around starting trends.

The girl yelling to me was Monique, a Black girl whose mom used to be the girlfriend of a notorious rapper in Los Angeles. Monique was the Bling Clique's ringleader, and you couldn't help but like her. There was no second-guessing anything Monique said or did; she spoke her truth at all times.

"What you reading there, girl?" she asked, strutting over.

"The autobiography of Malala Yousafzai."

"Malala what? Okay, now you makin' me sorry I asked."

I laughed. Monique was a trip.

"You doin' okay?" she asked, a little more serious. "Haven't seen you on the social scene for a while. I was getting worried."

Monique had a thing for Jake, but he never gave her a second glance. It hit her hard when he died. She even offered to pay for the funeral, which I declined. I nodded in answer, not interested in getting too deep. I preferred to stew in my misery rather than share it with the world. "I'm good, thanks."

She shifted into the seat beside me, and the next thing I knew, a hundred-dollar bill was stuffed between the pages of Malala's book. My mind immediately went to the place where I dissected things that seemed at odds with each other. In this case, the crisp hundred-dollar bill from a rich, young, American schoolgirl inside a book about a poor girl who was almost killed because she wanted an education.

"You need to help a girl out," Monique said. "Miss DeGracia wants her five-hundred-word essay. It's so out of the blue it's crazy. Anyway, I know you're not doing that anymore, but please, Anela, for old times' sake?"

"Actually, I'm getting back into it. That's kind of why I'm here."

"You're a lifesaver," she said. "I'll make sure to shoot some business your way. Just be sure to do mine first, okay?"

"Cool, thanks," I said. "What subject did you pick?"

"Subject? What are you talking about?"

"Monique, your social studies essay. I need to know what it's about, the subject."

"Oh, that. It's the image of perfection in advertising or something like that," she said. "Like, yeah, I ain't gonna buy blush or mascara from an ugly girl, you know what I'm saying?"

"Did you pick a topic that screams you or what?" I said.

Monique screamed with laughter. "Riiight?"

I peeked at the hundred-dollar bill. I couldn't fathom someone walking around with so much money to spend on trivial stuff. "Also, I don't have change," I said. "But I'll give it to you later."

"I'm not looking for change, Anela. Bury that pride of yours and chill. Do me this fave so I can get a C and make Daddy proud."

"Fine. But I'll do your next essay for free. Deal?"

"Ugh, whatever. Sure. And, girl, dial it down with the big words in the essay, okay? Last thing I need is Miss DeGracia getting suspicious. All I need is a C."

"Okay. I'll give it to you in the morning. Thanks, Monique."

That was her cue to return to the Bling Clique, but she lingered. She looked me up and down, scratching her cheek with perfectly manicured nails.

"We gotta do something about your look, babe," she said. "What do you have against a little dab of lip gloss? And that hair. You know how many girls would kill for that hair? You walk around like you stuck your finger in a socket, girl."

Did I mention how hard it was to dislike Monique? She pulled my appearance apart, and all I could do was laugh. I knew she didn't have a mean cell in her body.

"Shut up," I said. "It's just not my vibe."

"You're telling me. But listen, anytime you decide to glam up, come see me. I have clothes stored away from when I was still flat as a pancake. They'd fit you fine. And I could take you to my hairdresser. He could straighten your hair and turn you into a queen."

"I'm no queen."

Monique patted my cheek. "But you could be. I just want you to know you have options. You have my number."

And with that, she made her way back to the Bling Clique. I peeked over at the football players' table to gauge how many had figured out they needed my writing services. My gaze connected with Troy, Jake's best friend since middle school, even though they hailed from different sides of the tracks. Troy had texted me a few times after the funeral to see how I was doing, but I didn't engage. Just like I couldn't watch some of the spoof videos Jake and I had made or go to the football games.

Troy nodded slightly, which told me all I needed to know. My phone dinged with his text.

"You back in business?" he asked.

"Yes."

"Hang tight."

Troy had my back. I saw him lean in to conspire with his friends.

I started reading *Malala* between bites of meatloaf and mashed potatoes. The food was bland, but it stopped my tummy from rumbling.

Twenty minutes later, Troy slid a list of four names, their topics, and two hundred dollars in front of me.

"I figure you ought to charge more," he said. "I made it fifty for every essay."

"Wow, thanks," I said. I wanted to hug him, to feel that camaraderie we used to have. Troy never minded when I went to the movies with him and Jake; he'd been totally cool with it. I felt bad for ignoring him.

"I'm sorry I never texted back before," I mumbled, unsure if it even made a difference at this point.

"I understand," he said. "You were in a lot of pain . . . Hey, we're playing a big game Friday night. You should come."

I stared at him, the air whooshing out of me.

I could never watch a football game again. Not without reliving that moment when Jake was tackled on the field and never got up again. A fluke, they called it. A horrible accident. His head connected with the ground at an angle that snapped his neck and severed his spinal cord. He didn't even make it to the hospital. I tried to wipe the memory away, but I could still see it—the moment Jake's soul disconnected from his body. Every time I closed my eyes, I heard the distant, horrified yells, the ambulance. And the terrible silence after that.

My psyche took a few steps back from Troy. "I can't. I'm busy Friday night."

Troy picked up on my turmoil. He touched my shoulder. "I gotcha. It's all good."

"I'll give you the essays in the morning," I said. "Tell the guys I said thanks."

"Yep," Troy said with a little laugh. "I think they owe you thanks, but sure, I'll tell them. You stay cool. Later, A."

I forced a smile and watched Troy go back to his table, but a chill ran down my spine. No one but Jake had ever called me "A." I waffled between getting annoyed at Troy and letting it go because it wasn't like he was out to hurt me. I wore my grief like an open wound. One wrong word, and I was reeling back to that field, watching Jake die again. Something had to give. I prayed it would happen soon.

I stopped by Miss DeGracia's office, but she wasn't there. I went in anyway. For the first time, I noticed a small, framed picture on her desk: her Harvard graduation photo. *She went to Harvard???* She didn't tell me that. In the photo, she stood between her parents. They looked so proud, and she smiled like the world lay at her feet. Her background validated what Jake always said: where there's a will, there's a way. I wrote Miss DeGracia a quick note and folded forty dollars inside: Guess I'm going. Thank you. Anela XO.

· · ·

For the first time in two months, I was reluctant to leave school. This was where I felt alive, where my mind was challenged and my future came together like a complicated puzzle. If I actually participated—if I put the work in, which I felt up to doing again—what could stop me?

Outside, I strolled through the hordes of students whose moms were waiting at the gate in their shiny SUVs. Even if I wasn't the only kid going home to my lousy neighborhood, I was the only one who took the city bus back. The school bus tended to get rowdy, and the kids would tease me for being "the brainiac from the hood." It felt like a snub rather than a compliment. Taking the city bus involved less anxiety.

The bus wheezed and lurched down the road, spitting billows of smoke in its wake. I always sat up front, next to the window. I'd watch the world outside as it shifted from affluent suburbs to low-income housing. Today, I stopped looking. It was too depressing. I'd read or do homework instead.

Going *to* school from my neighborhood was a different story. That was the route I wanted my life to take: putting the miserable part behind me and heading for prosperity. Comparing a simple bus route to my life felt silly, but Jake would have been impressed with how I adjusted my outlook.

Once home, the essays kept me busy until midnight. Doing research, looking at topics from every angle, asking questions, and arguing the answers felt great. Jake once said I'd make a good lawyer because things always got busy inside my head.

Sometime after midnight, I heard Mom shuffling down the hallway toward her bedroom. She worked the night shift at a nursing home, basically cleaning up after the mess everyone else made during the day. Weeks earlier, I'd told her a lunch lady position was opening up soon at school. It paid more than her current job and had decent working hours. I even brought home an application form, but it remained on the kitchen counter, untouched.

The shuffling stopped outside my bedroom door, followed by a soft knock.

My first thought was that I'd done something wrong and she wanted to yell at me. I racked my mind. Did I leave a dirty dish in the sink? Forget to switch off the bathroom light? We mostly stayed out of each other's way, and I was super conscientious about keeping the apartment spotless. But there was no other reason for her to knock on my door.

There was another knock. "Anela?" she called.

"Yeah?" I said, trying to sound sleepy and hoping she'd go away.

"Can I come in?"

CHAPTER 4

I tried to shake off the tension creeping under my skin.

I once asked Jake why she targeted me, what I had done to make her hate me so much. Jake sat me down and said he could tell me a story to explain some of it, even though that wouldn't make it any better.

When Jake was still a baby, our parents' marriage was already falling apart. Mom scraped together all her courage and decided to divorce Dad, then return to school and become a nurse like she'd always wanted to be. It was all worked out. She would move in with her parents, and she and Dad agreed to share custody of Jake.

Then she found out she was pregnant with me. I was the reason she couldn't go back to school. The reason she was forced to go back to Dad. The reason her life turned into the crapshoot it was. At least, that's the way she saw it. The silent accusation was embedded in her eyes every time she looked at me.

Jake repeatedly assured me that none of it was my fault. I wasn't the reason Mom turned into a bitter, angry woman who couldn't accept the circumstances she'd created for herself. She needed to pile all her frustration and hate onto someone. I was defenseless, and that made me the perfect target. When Jake was old enough to realize what was happening, he became my parent, friend, defender, and biggest supporter. I didn't doubt for a second that without him, the weight of Mom's hate might have pushed me to my own downfall. I became wary of her and went out of my way to please her. But I was past hoping for friendship; I just wanted to avoid her wrath. Now here she was, outside my bedroom door, and all I felt was fear.

Mom knocked again. "I need your help with something." It didn't sound like she was looking for a fight. She sounded tired.

"Sure, come in."

She crept inside, still in her scrubs and holding the job application. She looked around the room in wonder, as if seeing it for the first time. It was small, but I made good use of the space, though some of my books were spilling off the rickety bookcase onto the floor. I had a collage of people I admired on the wall—people who'd made the world a better place in their own way, big or small. And for my fifteenth birthday, Jake bought me fairy lights that I strung up along the ceiling, giving the whole room a magical vibe.

"Wow," Mom said. "This looks really nice."

I was stunned. She'd seen the room many times before, and I'd had the lights up for ten months. For a fleeting moment, I wondered if she was on drugs or had bumped her head.

"You should move into Jake's room," she said. "You'll have more space for a small desk. And your window won't face traffic."

I was speechless and just let her sudden friendliness soak in.

"I was thinking about that," I finally said. "Yeah, maybe sometime in the future."

I didn't want to tell her that Jake's room had become my shrine, the place I went to when I needed to reflect and quiet my mind. Even with Jake gone, his room was filled with love. The only thing that kept me from going off the deep end was sitting on his bed and reading all the quotes we'd painted on the walls over the years. Quotes brimming with pain, love, and hope, but mostly inspiration.

"I'll help pack up Jake's stuff," she said. "It won't take long."

"No!" I said more harshly than I intended. "You can't pack up his stuff."

Removing everything from Jake's room would be like cutting out my soul. That small space had been our sanctuary when it all went to hell around us.

Mom's expression remained nonplussed. "It's okay, Anela. I won't touch his stuff. I understand."

This was a different woman than the Mom I knew. I tried to reason it out in my mind, but it occurred to me that being suspicious of her behavior might be the same thing she did with me. So I took a deep breath and went with the flow.

"It's just too soon," I said carefully. "Packing up his stuff would disappear him forever."

Mom nodded, the pain of losing her son in her eyes. I felt the unexpected urge to hug her and soothe the ache in her heart, but the invisible wall remained strong between us. She looked at the paper in her hand.

"So, I filled out the application, but there's a couple of things you could help me with. You write better than me."

I moved the laptop and books away to make room for her on the bed. "I'll clean up before I go to school," I said.

"It's okay, baby, it's fine. It's not that messy."

She'd never called me "baby," and her favorite hobby was to chastise me for anything she considered "messy." It could be a crumb on the kitchen counter or shoes that weren't lined up perfectly, side by side.

I studied her. The usual inflexible lines around her mouth had made way for a little smile, and her penetrating stare had softened to motherly concern. *Is she on something?* I wondered again. We were surrounded by drug dealers selling prescription-type stuff on the street. I'd seen it and heard the neighbors complain about it.

I swept my qualms aside. *Why ruin this moment?* It could be a new beginning for Mom and me. Maybe we could put all this misery behind us and start over. Nothing would have made Jake happier than seeing Mom be nice to me. I smiled.

"So, what is it you need help with?" I asked.

"Here, where it asks to explain why I think I'd be good at the job."

Suddenly I was the teacher, and my mom was the student.

"Well," I said, "tell me in your words why you think you'd be good at it."

"I'm good at going along with orders, and as you know, there's nothing I like more than following rules. Everything has to be just so."

"Okay," I said, "but a lunch lady is all about the kids and meeting their wants and needs food-wise. You raised two kids. You should say that and add that it's important to consider nutrition when preparing tasty meals."

Mom stared at me blankly, the little smile still in place. "Do I tell them I was responsible for the death of one of my kids?"

The shock coursed through my body, stealing my breath. It was so unexpected, especially now, here. "Please don't do this," I begged. "Why would you even say that?"

There was a long, sad moment as she shifted her focus to the Nelson Mandela poster on the wall, with one of his famous quotes at the bottom:

"WE ASK OURSELVES, WHO AM I TO BE BRILLIANT, GORGEOUS, TALENTED, FABULOUS? ACTUALLY, WHO ARE YOU NOT TO BE? . . . YOUR PLAYING SMALL DOES NOT SERVE THE WORLD."

Jake had bought me that poster two years before. It took center stage on my wall, and you couldn't miss it when you walked in the door. Now Mom stared at it like all life's answers were right there on Mandela's beautiful face. When she spoke, her voice was so soft I had to lean in to make out the words.

"Dad started training Jake to play football when he could barely walk. It was like he lived through Jake, molding Jake into the professional player he could never be himself. Jake wasn't smart like you. I knew the one way out of this life for all of us was for Jake to get into professional football. So I went along with Dad, pushing Jake as hard as I could. I never asked him if it was what he wanted. I should have, but I never did."

I steeled myself. This was one moment where I couldn't show any resentment. I couldn't admit that in some ways I blamed my parents for Jake's death. He wasn't stoked to play football; he did it because he knew it kept the family together.

"You can't blame yourself," I said. "It doesn't do any good. It doesn't help anyone."

Mom patted my cheek gently. It was such an unfamiliar gesture that I almost ducked like a slap was coming. She noticed, even though I tried to hide it, and tears pooled in her eyes.

"What have I done to you?" she asked. "I didn't treat you right, baby."

"Let's just fill in the application, okay?" I said quickly. I didn't know where this conversation was going, and she was acting so out of character. Another thought crossed my mind. *Should I even let her apply for a job at my school?* It would be one more thing to worry about every day. She was unpredictable; one kid giving her lip might put her over the edge.

"You have every reason to hate me, I know," she said.

"I don't hate you."

"I wouldn't blame you if you did."

"Let's fill in the application," I insisted. "It's late. I need to sleep."

"I didn't mean to bother you. Go to sleep then."

"No, it's fine. The sooner you get the application in, the better." *Why do I have to explain that to her?* Anger grew inside me. She wanted to come in here at this time of night, maybe high on something, and pretend the last fifteen years never happened? I struggled to keep composed and prevent the rage from winning out.

Jake always said rage was a sign of an imbalance inside you because something on the outside was beyond your control. And if you found out what was off balance, you were halfway to quelling the rage.

I took a deep breath and forced myself to get perspective. The sooner we completed the application, the sooner Mom would leave me alone. When I glanced up, our gazes locked. She probably recognized herself in me, just younger and not yet railroaded by life. I realized she hadn't come in here to fill out the application. She was here to make amends. To gauge my willingness to accept her stepping back into my life. It was asking a lot, and she knew it. I felt drained already.

"You need to sleep," she said and stood up. "We can do the application tomorrow."

"Okay," I said, relieved.

She hesitated at the door. "Can I say one thing?" she asked.

"You know you can."

"Don't make the same mistakes I made. All it takes is one stupid slipup. You're young. You're smart. Work with that. Save the boys for later. It's all about choice. Choose with your head and not your heart."

And then she was gone, closing the door behind her. It was after midnight, and I was exhausted, but my mind wouldn't rest.

Dissecting my feelings was a job I didn't want to take on just then, so I decided to read *I Am Malala* until I felt sleepy. Two hours later, my eyelids started to get heavy. As I drifted off to sleep, my last thought was a quote from the book: *"Once I had asked God for one or two extra inches in height, but instead he made me as tall as the sky, so high that I could not measure myself."*

CHAPTER 5

So, like I said, today was the first day in two months I woke up feeling that the future held promise, just waiting to be discovered. I wasn't about to question this new feeling, for fear it might disappear.

Before I left my room, my phone dinged with a text from Tamara. I thought my eyes were deceiving me.

"Hi. I want to chat with you please."

I didn't text back immediately. *Why would Tamara want to speak to me all of a sudden?* We hadn't spoken in five months, and for good reason. I thought we were best friends, until she found out I had a crush on her brother, Shiloh.

"My mom is okay about me being friends with you," she said one day at lunch. "But there's no way she'd allow Shiloh to date someone who lives where you do."

Maybe it was the way she said it, casually labeling me without thinking twice. I never expected Shiloh to crush back. He was a grade higher than me, and being the great guy he was, he could pick and choose who he wanted to date.

We once had a moment when he was running for school president and his "campaign" needed a slogan. It happened at a Friday sleepover at Tamara's house, which was gigantic; the trip from her bedroom to the kitchen for a glass of milk was a hike. On the way, I passed a room where a few boys and a girl sat around a table, planning Shiloh's campaign strategy.

They were trying to come up with a campaign slogan, but they were all talking over each other. As far as I could tell, each idea was worse than the last. I dared to enter the lion's den.

"You're making it too complicated," I said. "Make the slogan easy to remember. Keep it short. Make the words rhyme. Something like 'Go with Shiloh.'"

One boy smiled and nodded at Shiloh. "Okay, I love that."

The girl looked me up and down, all attitude topped off with a sneer. "Who asked you? I mean, who are you, even?"

Shiloh glared at her. "Ingrid, what the heck?" Then he looked at me. "Excuse my rude friend here, Anela."

"You mean campaign manager," Ingrid shot back. "Oh, wait, this is Tamara's friend your mom told me about."

I wasn't going to hang around for more of that, so I made myself scarce. I immediately regretted not standing my ground, but picking a fight with a stranger just because she rubbed me the wrong way wasn't worth it. *Why did she have to be that way, though?* Then I got lost on my way to the kitchen. Imagine a house big enough to get lost in. It was so not the world I was used to. Our whole apartment could fit inside their living room.

"Hey, Anela!" Shiloh called out as I marched down the hallway. I swung around, feeling a flutter in my stomach as he caught up with me. He ran a hand through his mop of blond hair. It was sweet seeing him a little flustered. "Look, I'm sorry about that," he said. "Ingrid is good at what she does, but she's not exactly a people person."

"It's fine," I said. "I don't really care. That's on her, not me."

I hoped that sounded confident.

Shiloh grinned. "That's a pretty good attitude to have. Can't say I'd be that nice about it myself."

"I've learned when to let things go and when they're worth fighting for. Ingrid isn't worth it."

Shiloh didn't seem in any rush to leave. As a matter of fact, he leaned against the wall, like he was getting comfortable for a few minutes of conversation. "I like what you said in there," he told me. "The slogan. I mean, you came up with that on the spot."

"I wouldn't say on the spot. I had at least ten seconds to think about it."

Shiloh laughed, and for a moment we found ourselves in this little bubble, comfortably sharing space without having to make small talk. His gaze never left me.

"You should go out for school government," he said. "I'm sure if you decided to fight for an issue, you'd represent it well."

"Oh no, I hate public speaking," I told him. "Do you know people fear that more than death?"

"No way," Shiloh said.

"Way."

"Well, you could always work behind the scenes," he said. "I'd love to have someone like you to help with my campaign. If you wanted to, of course."

The world blurred, and my cheeks grew hot. I was sure that blushing like a lovestruck teenager would all but announce to Shiloh that I had a crush on him. He was tall with hazel eyes. There was no doubt he was headed for greatness. You could see it in the way he carried himself. And asking me to work his campaign? A big fat YES was on the tip of my tongue when Shiloh's dad interrupted us. He slapped Shiloh on the back. "Don't you have a campaign to run, Shi?"

Shiloh straightened up fast, his confidence evaporating before my eyes. He seemed to be afraid of his father.

"Yes, sir, I do. Thanks again, Anela. Good night."

"Good night, Shiloh," I said and stood there, stunned. In an instant, the atmosphere had changed from easygoing to tense and edgy.

"Why don't you go up to Tamara?" his father said. "Anna, is it?"

It wasn't like I hadn't been introduced to him about ten times before.

"It's Anela. Good night." I stalked down another hall, not knowing where I was going. When I found the stairs, I climbed them as quickly as I could. Tamara was putting on glitter nail polish when I stormed into her bedroom. She waved me to the bed and patted the spot next to her.

"Where have you been? Come, let me do your nails too!"

I held out my hands, and Tamara immediately dipped the little brush in the bottle and applied the glitter polish to my nails.

"Your dad still has trouble remembering my name," I said. "What's up with that?"

Tamara smiled, but there was a glint of angst in her eyes. "Forget about him. Hey, let's do our toenails too."

That was the last time I went to Tamara's house. Two days later was when she said her mom would never let Shiloh date an impoverished girl like me. I didn't even finish my lunch when she said it. I just got up and left. She texted me for a few days after, demanding I tell her what I was so upset about. I finally texted back: "It's not that your mom thinks I'm not good enough for Shiloh. It's that you thought it was cool to tell me that. Your prejudice runs deep, T. It makes me wonder why you're friends with me in the first place. Is it because your mom thought it might win you points at school? Just leave me alone."

After that, Tamara refused to acknowledge me. *Probably experiencing her own resentment at being dissed by a "poor" girl*, I thought bitterly. I also have roots in immigrant plantation workers in old Hawaii from my dad, and Mom was the black sheep of her family. My resentment grew into this unmanageable ramble of negative thoughts I desperately tried to push away. It was hard to let go of the anger.

Then, when Jake died, nothing else mattered. I stopped nurturing my anger toward Tamara as my focus turned to coping with the raw, empty feeling that consumed me. I used to lie in bed at night, listening to Jake walk around in his room, the ancient wood floor creaking slightly under his weight. That sound made me feel safe and lulled me to sleep for many years.

Now the nightly silence and the cold knowledge of Jake's death overshadowed everything else. There was simply no space left for my anger at Tamara. It had become a nonsensical emotion with no foundation, no roots, nothing to make it grow or even survive.

Tamara's text took me back to that final conversation in the cafeteria. It felt like a lifetime ago. Had I judged her too harshly? We'd been friends for two years, and the story of our first meeting still made me smile.

We met during our freshman year, at Brooklyn's annual combined-sports event, where a few friendly high schools competed in informal games. I'd seen Tamara around school, but we didn't move in the same circles, so there was no connection.

After the field hockey game, which Tamara had played in, four girls from another school ganged up on her in the hall. They didn't take their loss against Brooklyn High well and, being typical bullies, picked a fight with her. Their accusations didn't even make sense. Not that it mattered.

The biggest girl shoved Tamara against the wall and yelled in her face. Tamara looked terrified and begged them to stop. When the big girl shoved Tamara again, she started to cry. I didn't care why this was happening anymore. I had to do something to stop it.

"What's going on here?" I said, trying to sound tough. "You're being real jerks."

The big girl swung around, then she stomped over and got in my face. "If I wanted your opinion, I'd be asking you!" she yelled. "But I don't remember asking!" She turned to her buddies. "Did any of you hear me ask for her opinion?"

Of course, they all shook their heads, and I wondered if stepping into their lane was such a great idea. But one look at Tamara, and I squared my shoulders and got right back in the bully's face.

"Well, I decided to give it to you anyway," I said. "What are you going to do about it?"

Tamara looked at me like I was her savior, so I had to keep up the brave charade. But they would've wiped the floor with me in a physical fight; I decided to put the big girl down verbally because I was good with words, and you fight with what you have.

"Listen," I said, "you probably struggle with a sense of inadequacy.

I mean, as a complete stranger who doesn't know you, that's what I get from this. And for some dumb reason, you think bullying someone else makes you seem like an alpha female and in charge of your life, which it doesn't. Because you're just a stupid, insecure girl who doesn't realize that one day you'll run into someone bigger and meaner than you are. So I suggest you take your ugly face and your super-uncool friends and get out of here. If you want, I'll count to three."

I don't think anyone had ever spoken to her like that. She and her pals shared a few confused glances. One of them shrugged nonchalantly. "Let's go," she said. "Before these two babies go crying to their mommies."

Tamara and I watched them leave, and Tamara turned to me with a huge smile. "That was awesome!" she said. "You are the coolest person I've ever met. Thank you."

"That went way better than I thought it would," I said. "But you're welcome."

"I'm Tamara."

"I'm Anela." And just like that, we were best friends. Until we weren't.

Her new text forced my pride to step back. I'd never given her a chance to explain herself. How could I judge things when I didn't know both sides?

I took it as a sign that the day I woke up feeling like a new life was out there was the same day she texted me. I texted back: "You going on the class trip today?"

"No, I'm taking a few sick days."

"R U okay?"

"It's complicated. Possible for you to come visit me after school?"

I was in a daze. What was going on with Tamara? I sensed a panicky vibe in her text, but maybe I was super sensitive about anything bad happening to people I loved.

Pushing whatever wisp of resentment remained to the side, I texted back: "Of course. I'll come around after the class trip. What's going on?"

"Better to tell you in person."

"KK. Text you when I'm on the way."

I received two hearts and a smiley-face emoji. I opted not to worry until she told me exactly what was happening and sent her a smiley emoji back. It was a small step forward, but it felt good, so I went with it.

As I printed out the five essays I'd written, my ears pricked up. I heard Mom moving around the apartment, probably getting ready for work. For a moment, I felt nervous about facing her because the dynamic between us had shifted. Knowing there was a vulnerable woman inside Mom's tough shell put me more at ease, but that didn't mean I could stop walking on eggs.

I glanced in the small mirror beside my bed to see if I passed for presentable. Something in my face had changed over the past months, and it took me a moment to figure out what it was: I was losing my baby fat, which my Hawaiian grandmother called *momona*. My plump cheeks had slimmed down, making my lips look fuller, but not in a bad way. Of course, my hair remained out of control. All I could do was take it back into a bushy ponytail.

Monique was right; I could probably do more with my appearance. I didn't own any makeup, though, so that would have to wait for another time. Tamara had tried to make my face up once, but it tickled, and I was giggling so much she gave up.

Mom was in our small kitchen, buttering toast she'd arranged on a plate. She greeted me with a mug of coffee and a smile.

"I didn't know if you took milk. Sugar?" she said.

"Milk, two sugars," I replied. "But I'm not fussy."

"Lucky guess, then—same as me," she said.

The fact that Mom didn't know how I took my coffee was a small thing, but it put a light on how broken our relationship was. In two weeks I'd be sixteen years old, and this was the first time she'd made me a cup of coffee. I scraped that thought from my mind. No use dwelling on the past. Like Jake always said, look forward, move forward.

I wasn't hungry, but I forced down a piece of toast, doing my share to work toward a better relationship. This was obviously Mom's effort to bring her part. She leaned against the counter, arms folded, staring at me. But I didn't detect hostility.

"You doing anything special today?" she asked.

Though Mom's sudden interest in my life was jarring, I cast my suspicions aside and gave her the benefit of the doubt.

"There's a class trip to the State House at noon. We're gonna watch a live session."

"Oh, I didn't know that was a thing," she said. "That anyone could just go there."

"Sure, it's open to the public," I said. "Can't wait. It's going to be great."

"Look at you, perking up like that," she said. "I wonder if you know just how pretty you are."

"Oh, stop," I said with my mouth full of toast. "Monique says I look like I put my finger in a socket with this hair." Crumbs flew all over the place as I spoke. I flicked a nervous glance at Mom, waiting for the scold, but she was laughing. It was infectious, so I started laughing too. And the more she laughed, the more I laughed. Tears were running down our cheeks. A few crumbs got stuck in my throat, and it took sucking down the entire mug of coffee to strangle my cough.

"You okay?" she asked, still giggling.

I nodded, amazed at this side of her I'd never seen before.

"I'm going to be late," I said and grabbed my backpack. "See you tonight? We can finish writing that application."

She smiled. "Sure, baby. That would be good."

Halfway out the front door, I remembered the essays were still on the kitchen counter. I swung back, and Mom was shaking a white pill from a tiny baggie.

I froze. She looked up, startled. Our sentences crossed over.

"It's just for my headache—"

"I forgot my papers—"

I nearly fell over my feet to grab the papers and leave. I'd have the long trip to school to think about what I'd just seen.

CHAPTER 6

My analytical mind was a blessing, sure. But at times it felt like a punishment in its tendency to contemplate things to death. I didn't know what to make of Mom taking a pill. But I did know that was no headache pill. For one, headache pills didn't come in suspicious little baggies. I'd seen enough drug deals in the neighborhood to know where those kinds of baggies came from.

On my way down the broken hall stairs, I passed Moses, the "manager" of our apartment complex. He was between forty and fifty, with a persistent vapor of menace drifting around him.

"Hey, Anela, yo' momma home?" he asked, like we were friends or something.

"What do you want from her?" I demanded, despite knowing I'd miss the bus if I engaged with this misfit.

"Why you so uptight?" He shook his head as if this interaction were spoiling his otherwise magnificent day. "Need ta collect for rest'a the rent. Ya know how that goes."

"How much do we still owe?" I asked.

"One fifty 'n change,"

Moses was a thorn in my side who added to my anxiety without trying. Jake had always been a buffer, protecting me from the lewd glances Moses pitched my way. I suspected the gun in Jake's vault had a lot to do with Moses and the intimidating strays he hung around with in our building. Weekends were the worst. If there was a party and a fight broke out, you'd find Moses at ground zero. The cops did their rounds but rarely intervened except to break things up if some fools got into a serious scrap.

I backed against the wall as Moses closed in on me. The stink on him made my stomach turn. Jake wasn't there to help, so I was on my own.

"Wait here. I'll get the money," I said, panic rushing out of me like vomit.

I ran back into the apartment, passed Mom in the kitchen, and ducked into Jake's room. After forty dollars for the class trip, I still had one sixty from yesterday's essay payments in the vault. I took the money out, my fingers scraping the gun. For a mesmerizing second, I wondered what it would feel like to hold it on someone like Moses, to have that kind of power over them. My heart raced. *Why would I even go there in my mind?* Even if the gun was out of sight, its presence haunted me.

Mom stood in the same spot, staring at nothing. Just like when I came in. We locked eyes. She must have read the silent accusation because she held out a hand to make amends. But I was late for the city bus and didn't want to waste more time figuring out how to handle this. So I just said, "I'm paying the rest of the rent. Don't let Moses tell you otherwise."

She barely nodded before I dashed out again, accidentally slamming the door behind me. I stuffed the money in Moses's hands.

"Count it, please," I instructed him, itching to get to school. While he did that, I snuck out my phone and took a video of the transaction. This wasn't my first dealing with Moses, and the video was my receipt. As it was his nature to stir things up, he didn't like when things went smoothly. He took his time counting. Eventually he mumbled, "Fine," and I watched him stumble back to his section of the building.

I sprinted down the street with an uneasy feeling in my stomach and my mind running a thousand miles a minute. The bus was already leaving the stop, but the driver hit the brakes when he saw me trying to catch up. It seemed like my whole life was me running and trying to catch up. When I reached the bus, I took deep breaths like Jake taught me. Deep, even breaths until my body succumbed to a calm that spread from my toes to my head. But it wasn't working today. The brewing storm seemed to grow instead of settling down.

The only open seat was next to an older lady neatly dressed in a coat and scarf. It was pretty miserable outside, but the bus was as warm and cozy as a city bus could get. The moment I sat, the older lady took out a sandwich, laid a tissue on her lap, and nibbled away.

"Breakfast. I hope you don't mind," she said.

I shook my head no, but whatever she had on that sandwich smelled good, and my stomach growled. I pretended not to notice and stared out the dirty window like my life depended on it. Next thing I knew, the lady had spread a tissue across my lap and put the other half of the sandwich on that.

"My husband," she said. "He's the one who makes me eat breakfast and then packs a sandwich to eat on my way to work as well. Keeps me from getting hungry later, he says. I think he wants me round to keep the other men from looking too long. Eat up. It's roast beef."

"Are you sure?" I asked, secretly hoping she was very sure.

"Oh, definitely," she said. "They have glazed donuts at work, and I dare anyone to refuse a fresh donut with their morning coffee."

"Wow, thank you," I mumbled and devoured the sandwich. My stomach didn't complain.

"My name is Marlene," the woman said.

"I'm Anela," I replied with a mouthful of food. "Pleased to meet you."

I must have looked like I was starving, because she scratched around in her oversized purse and hauled out an apple. "It's been in my bag since yesterday, so I'd give it a rinse before eating it."

I gratefully accepted the apple. "You're really kind, thank you," I said, wondering why this stranger was so good to me. She must have read my mind.

"You remind me of my daughter," she explained. "You have the same smile."

"What's her name?" I asked.

"Lina. She was named after her grandmother, my mom."

I heard the affection in her voice. What I wouldn't give for a tenth of that from my mom. "I bet you're really proud of Lina," I said.

Marlene brushed the few crumbs off her lap, folded the tissue neatly, and buried it in a pocket of her purse. "Lina died one year ago," she said.

I almost choked on my last bite at Marlene's confession. "I'm so sorry" was all I managed to say.

"We tried our best to get her help, but the drugs had a fierce grip on her. One day she took too much and slipped away. She was only seventeen, still a baby in our eyes. The grief stayed with me for so long that I almost gave up on life. Then, a few days ago, I started a new shift, and this was the bus I took. I saw you get on, and when you smiled, it was like looking at my Lina again. I knew God put you in my path to help heal some of the pain."

There was no stopping the tears burning my eyes. I was willing to take on all this woman's pain if that would give her some small comfort. I took her hand and held it until we reached her stop.

"Maybe I'll see you again, Anela," she said. "Until then, stay safe, you hear? And remember, the Lord always has your back."

It left me in a daze, this unexpected encounter filled with so much love. But I couldn't keep my mind from wandering back to Mom popping that pill. *Is she using rent money to buy drugs?* I wondered. She'd always been super dependable about getting rent settled up. Jake and I would help with food and heating bills, but she always made the rent herself. *And suddenly she's one fifty short?*

No doubt Mom was using, but I had no idea what kind of pills they were. I wasn't angry as much as I felt betrayed. *So, that's what it takes for her to be nice to me.* I choked down my emotions, getting a firm grip on them and trying to keep Jake's voice alive. "You're in charge of your thoughts," he'd say. "How things affect you is up to you."

This morning, I woke up with a new view on life. If I let myself become engulfed by negative thoughts, that was on me. Running into

Marlene had been auspicious, like she was an angel sent to steer me back on the right course. I put the brakes on my destructive thought process, waiting for my heart to stop pounding and the discomfort in my stomach to dull. It allowed me to analyze the situation from a distance.

It wasn't my responsibility to tell Mom how to conduct her life. She was a grown woman who knew the difference between right and wrong. Even if she didn't seem to care.

Still, I was shocked that Mom thought more about getting high than what would happen to me if she got busted. I had no choice but to live with her. There was no way out of that except foster care, which was where I'd wind up if she got in that kind of trouble. And I only had to listen to neighborhood stories to know about the horrors of foster care. To be honest, I could look after myself just fine. Jake and I practically raised ourselves anyway. All I needed was a safe place to go at night. The apartment was all I knew, and it was relatively safe. But paying rent was an issue. I could pay the utility bills since they were low. And I had school for food. But rent was too much for me to carry alone.

The anger had taken root inside me again, and I figured I might as well deal with it instead of burying it. I had to reason it into submission. For starters, I was bitter about having to cover the rest of the rent with money I'd earned. On the other hand, at least I had enough to pay. This time. My mind wandered to Malala's biography. That girl had to fight for something I took for granted, almost paying with her life, so I had no business whining about having to spend money I earned using my brain. Education was the one constant light in my existence and the only path to take if I wanted to rise instead of fall.

"When it all looks like it's going to pieces," Jake would say, "find that one thing, no matter how small, that's positive. Let that be your beacon."

So, that's what I did. I was surprised to find three things to feel good about. One was hearing Jake's voice again. The second was that no one was threatening my chance to jam my head full of knowledge. I once again looked forward to school, and as a bonus, there was the class trip to the State House. The third thing was meeting Marlene. I didn't know if I'd ever see her again, but I knew I'd never forget her.

• • •

At school, I found Troy with his buddies near the lockers, watching a video on someone's phone. When I tapped his arm, he pulled me into the circle to watch with them. "Look at this cat, A!" he laughed. "It's trying to catch the laser dot."

So, calling me "A" is going to be a thing. Fine, I thought. I had to admit it felt good to be social again. We all watched the video and shared a good laugh before I pulled Troy aside and handed him the pile of essays.

"Listen," I whispered, "if there are other essays to do, let me know, okay?" I didn't want anyone else to know how desperate I was for more business.

"You got it," Troy said.

"Thanks, T!" I replied.

"I see what you did there," he said, laughing. "You don't mind me calling you A?"

"Nope," I said, deciding it in the moment. "It reminds me of Jake."

"You doin' all right with money and whatnot?" he asked carefully. Troy was no stranger to my situation at home. He was Jake's best friend, and before Jake and I got "jobs," Troy would casually hand Jake gift cards he said "happened" to be lying around unused. It cut Jake deep, but he batted the humiliation aside because Troy was doing it out of love, and you could only subsist on ramen noodle cups for so long before your body revolted.

Though it was heartwarming that Troy still cared, I saw no reason to get into the harsh reality at home. I'm sure he had some idea. So I just nodded.

"It's fine. I deal," I said.

"Would you tell me if it wasn't?" he asked.

"It's all cool," I mumbled. "More essays would be good, though, so if you could keep your ear to the ground."

"Yup, I'm on it. You just take care of you."

The very moment I waved Troy a friendly goodbye, Shiloh walked past. Our eyes met briefly, but his gaze immediately found refuge on the floor. We hadn't spoken since that night at his house. Soon after, he dropped out of the campaign. I was as surprised as everybody else. He was an honor student, editor of the award-winning school paper, and captain of the water polo team. Running for school president seemed like the next logical step.

"Hey, Shiloh," I mumbled.

I thought my greeting would drift off unheard, but Shiloh swung around. I almost fell over my own feet with excitement.

CHAPTER 7

"Hey, Anela," he said, running his fingers through his hair in that familiar gesture. "How're you doing?"

I buried my clumsiness with a quick smile, but I stumbled over my words.

"It's all good. How's life treating you?"

I hated myself for being so awkward. Other girls in school always looked so cool and in charge when they interacted with boys. Flipping their hair, being coy, and generally acting like they didn't care, which supposedly made them more alluring. I couldn't even pull off a simple hello without making a fool of myself.

"Good, thanks," he started. "I . . . My family sent you a card. Did you get it?"

"Yeah, thanks. I was too much of a mess to respond to anyone. I'm sorry."

My stomach fluttered when our eyes met. It was so cliché. *Why do I feel like this with Shiloh?* I tried to argue with myself that it was his geekiness that intrigued me, but truthfully, Shiloh was one good-looking guy.

"No problem," he said. "Just wanted to make sure you got it."

I made a mental note to polish my social interaction skills. Because if there was a level for pathetic, this was it right here.

"Tamara texted me this morning," I said. "Is she okay?"

Shiloh nodded and shrugged. "Nobody tells me anything, so I assume it's all under control."

"Okay, it's just that she's been out sick, and—you know what, never mind."

"Hey, it's not like I don't care," Shiloh said. "I've tried to check in on her, but every time, she's asleep. My mom says she's fine, and I have no reason not to believe her. Then again, nobody ever really talks in our house."

I found that weird. Jake and I had created a bond because our parents were so disconnected from life. I knew Shiloh and Tamara weren't close, but I couldn't fathom not sharing any brother-sister bond whatsoever.

"It's okay. I'm seeing her later," I said, trying to make light of the moment. "I'll let you know how she's doing."

Being who he was, Shiloh smiled, all in on my stupid joke.

"That's funny," he said. "It's good to see the old Anela is back. You vanished there for a while."

I was amazed that Shiloh had noticed my antisocial act. A warm sensation suffused my heart, and I felt a little more optimistic about things. Shiloh didn't care what color my skin was. Or that I came from the other side of the tracks.

"I . . . So," I stuttered. "Last I saw, you were running for president. Then all of a sudden you weren't."

"Yup."

"Why?"

Shiloh shrugged carelessly, but I read it differently. That was a shrug that begged me not to question his decision because the real reason was too hard to mention. I didn't know whether to push. But of course I had to.

"I want to know," I said. "You can trust me. Who am I going to tell?"

"I realized it was too much to take on with schoolwork and being editor of the newspaper and the other stuff," he said. "That's all."

I didn't believe him for a second. Where I came from, it was survival of the sharpest, so you learned to read people. They hid their worries in various ways. Shiloh's voice gave him away.

"Okay then, don't tell me," I said glibly. Inside, I cringed at being so pushy.

But pushy had worked for Jake when he pressed me to free myself of turmoil.

There was a "gym" in the basement of our apartment building that consisted of a few barbells and a well-used punching bag. Jake would drag me down there and tell me to give a face to my anger and picture that face on the punching bag. I didn't want to, but Jake pushed until I dug out the rage and put a face to it. Then I hit the punching bag until my knuckles were red. I could hardly move the punching bag, but it was a good release, if temporary. And it worked well enough that I avoided stomach ulcers.

While my thoughts bounced around, something in Shiloh bent.

"You really want to know why I dropped out?" he asked. A bitter look warped his beautiful face. He tried to hold tight to his emotions, but the dam was cracking.

"You don't have to tell me," I said. "I'm sorry. I didn't mean to upset you—"

And then the dam broke. "It's because if I didn't win, my father would make my life miserable." His voice sounded like broken glass. "I made up an excuse to drop the campaign because I couldn't face that man's wrath if I lost. So there you have it. Happy now?"

My heart sank. I wanted more than anything to put my arms around Shiloh and tell him everything would be fine. Even if I didn't believe it myself. Some of Jake's philosophy had rubbed off on me, I guess.

"I'm on your side," I said. "You know that, right?"

"Yes, of course. I didn't mean to—"

"Shiloh, it's okay."

"Not really," he said softly. "It wasn't okay to take my frustrations out on you."

"I didn't take it like that," I said, soothing him. "It sounds like you need someone to talk to."

For a few moments, we were in our safe space, finding comfort in each other's presence.

"And not that it matters," I said, "but I think you would have won. I really do. You have what it takes. Don't let anyone tell you otherwise."

"It's going to sound odd," he said, "but I didn't want to be school president."

"Seriously?" I asked. "Okay. Then why did you run?"

"Because my father wanted me to. I don't even know why I still try to make him happy. I'm like a dog begging for a few crumbs off the dinner table."

I wanted to tell Shiloh I had his back, but our safety bubble popped when the hallway started filling up with kids and a cacophony of noise. The moment was gone, and suddenly Shiloh looked ashamed.

"That was stupid," he said. "Forget I said anything. Just having a bad moment. I have to go. See you around, Anela."

"Sure," I said reluctantly. "Bye, Shiloh."

He waved quickly and hurried into the crowd. I stared after him, his confession weighing heavy on my mind. I couldn't help but compare our lives. I realized the only security wealth gave you was materialistic; brutal realities still controlled your spirit. Shiloh was imprisoned by circumstances, even if they were wrapped in gold. In a way, I was better off than he was because no one expected anything impressive from someone like me. I had nowhere to go but up. Way up.

CHAPTER 8

My attention was snatched away by Monique yelling from across the hall. "Hey, Anela girl! Wait up!"

I held out Monique's social studies essay as she sashayed over in her designer wear. Her lip gloss was so thick I could see my reflection. Her perfume hit my nostrils, and it was all I could do not to sneeze. *Is that what it takes to attract boys?* I wondered. Monique had the boys wrapped around her little finger and an incredible confidence in everything she did. It was hard to admit in my rebellious core, but I'd do anything to be as cool and self-assured as Monique.

She grabbed her essay and started reading, her lips moving along with the words. Then she tilted her head and looked at me. "I've never met a girl who could write like you," she said.

"It's a simple essay, Monique. Don't be impressed. It's nothing."

She laughed. "Listen to you, right up in my face. Having none of what I'm serving. I like that side of you, girl. Hey, have I told you about the party at my house Friday night?"

"Party?"

"Yeah, a party. You know, where people get together to have a good time?"

No one had ever invited me to a party. Jake had been invited to all of them, but since he thought they were just an excuse to drink and get stupid, he never went. Then he started going out a couple of nights a week, disappearing for a few hours, and I thought he'd given in to peer pressure. One night, I asked him how the party was, and he said it was fine. The following Monday at school, I found out there was no party. Finally, I figured out Jake must be seeing a girl.

"If you don't go to parties," I asked him once when he was getting ready to go out, "where are you off to for hours at a time?"

He styled his hair in the cracked bathroom mirror. "It's private, A. Give me a break."

"Just curious," I insisted. "I mean, this is a lot of effort to put in for your friends."

Jake laughed and gave me a nudge. "Mess with me all you like. I'm gonna have a good time."

"You in love?" I asked.

He didn't have to say anything; the answer was written in his eyes.

"You'll meet her soon," he promised. "For now, I just wanna spare her all the drama around here, if you know what I mean."

Of course I knew what he meant. Imagine bringing anyone into this house, where Dad got more obnoxious the more he drank—and he drank a lot—and Mom suppressed her emotions in a silent rage until she blew her top. Our family was way past dysfunctional. We were broken.

Jake never told me who the mystery girl was. At the funeral, I peered around at all the faces, wondering if she was there. His cell phone might have held some clues—if it hadn't disappeared somewhere between the football field and the hospital. It wasn't in his bag or his locker, and the hospital didn't have it. I was mad because it held so many of his memories, probably even ones he never shared with me. And I was petrified some stranger would discover Jake's secrets. I wanted to safeguard his legacy.

"Helloooo, Anela!" Monique snapped her fingers in front of me.

"Yes. Yes, I'll come to your party," I said.

Monique beamed like she'd just rescued an alley cat off the mean streets.

"You should come early so we can glam you up," she said. "And, girl, do I have the dress for you."

I let myself get caught up in Monique's plans to make me glamorous. It wasn't like I had anything in my tiny closet to wear to a party. I got most of my clothes from thrift stores, and my fashion sense was iffy. I liked comfortable clothes that defended against Boston's harsh winters. One time, Tamara insisted on buying me a cute party dress for my fifteenth birthday, so we went to the mall. I couldn't believe the prices.

"Who pays $125 for a flimsy little garment like this?" I asked.

"And who says 'flimsy little garment,' Anela, seriously?" she said. "This isn't even the designer stuff. Wait 'til you see *those* prices. Besides, I told you, it's my mom's card, and she doesn't care. Go nuts."

I lasted about ten minutes in that store before I wanted out. Lights flashing to the beat of blaring music made me feel claustrophobic and panicky.

"Let's go, please," I begged. "This place scares me."

Tamara laughed and pulled me to safety. "The same way I feel when you drag me to a bookstore."

We strolled around the mall, and Tamara insisted I pick out a gift at another store. I steered her to the Apple store and settled on a pair of earbuds to use with my laptop. To me, that was the perfect gift.

Birthdays were not celebrated at my house, at least not as I imagined other families celebrated theirs. There was no hoopla, no cake, no fuzzy birthday hug. Jake and I would go to the Chinese all-you-can-eat buffet for twelve dollars and catch a movie. That was our celebration. With my sixteenth birthday two weeks away, I couldn't imagine what it would be like without my brother.

In the hall, Monique was still in rescue mode, listing all the things we had to do to my appearance. She made it sound like one of those reality programs where they turn the ugly duckling into a princess after many exhausting hours of fussing and grooming. I watched a program like that with Tamara once and felt dumber afterward. Sure, it was uplifting, but it was way too shallow for me to get emotionally involved. I agreed with Jake that sometimes beauty was a mask that hid the ugly below the skin.

". . . and I'm definitely getting my hairdresser to work on that mop of yours," Monique chattered on. "He'll do his magic with you. Wish I had hair like yours, girl. I'd wear it like a crown. And don't worry about getting a ride back home Friday night, because I know that's exactly what you're tryin' to figure out while you starin' off into nothing."

"I'm not worried," I said. "The buses run until midnight."

Monique yanked me into a corner and shook her head dramatically. "You lost your mind, girl? No one goes ridin' a bus that time of night. You're staying over at my house. 'Kay?"

"I'll take an Uber if it makes you feel better," I said.

"Or I can just get our driver to take you home," Monique offered.

I decided to go with the flow. "Sure, that sounds great. Thank you," I said.

So that settled it. I would experience my first high school party, and I didn't have to worry about catching a bus in the middle of the night. I had to admit I was a little excited. I always felt left out when everyone was gossiping about who did what at which party. Someone always made a fool of themselves and ended up fully clothed in a swimming pool. It was usually innocent and silly, though at one point gossip spread about some boys who messed with an intoxicated girl. They weren't from our school, but a picture of the incident made the rounds on social media, and the police got involved. Jake had a long, serious talk with me, saying no boy should ever touch me without my consent.

"I kinda know that, Jake," I said. I loved my brother for always wanting to protect me, but sometimes the things he said were obvious.

"That includes getting yourself in situations where you might become vulnerable," he said.

"You mean getting drunk?" I asked. "I don't drink. I would never drink. I just have to look around here to see the damage that does."

"Don't dismiss this so quickly, A," Jake said. "It's easy to get sucked into the moment. Some people are ruthless, convincing you to do something you'd never do otherwise. All I'm sayin' is, watch out for those moments. They happen when you least expect them."

"Okay, okay," I assured him. "I'll be vigilant."

"Vigilant!" Jake said. "Big word for a little girl, but right on."

• • •

A few steps into my first class, it hit me that I didn't have my English assignment with me. I'd handed Troy the whole bunch of printouts without thinking to take mine. Of course, it had to happen in Mr. Lanfelt's class. I was already on thin ice with him; he took my slide from A to C student personally, like a slap in the face.

Mr. Lanfelt used to be an English professor at Yale. The question of why he was now a high school English teacher set all kinds of rumors loose. One was that he'd treated Yale's privileged students like ordinary people instead of as super special. All I knew was he was an alcoholic, and I suspected that had something to do with his Yale days being cut short. He wasn't hardcore like Dad yet, but the signs were there. The hand tremor in the morning; the antiseptic smell, as if gargling mouthwash could purify the stench of stale liquor; the red face and puffy eyes.

Early-morning classes with Mr. Lanfelt involved him lashing out at students who—he thought—didn't take his class seriously enough. His favorite thing to do was pick a particularly badly written paper and have its author read it to the class. Occasionally, he'd interrupt with snide remarks. This often delighted the other students, who were happy to escape the mocking session themselves.

Afternoon classes with Mr. Lanfelt took on a different tone. He was cool, engaging, and everyone's friend. By then the smell of alcohol lingered like an invisible shell around him, and there were no tremors in his hands—all telltale signs that Mr. Lanfelt had enjoyed a liquid lunch.

I once asked Jake why anyone would choose to destroy themselves with alcohol.

"People find solace in anything that dulls the pain," he said.

"Sometimes it's booze, other times drugs. And sometimes they'll chase that solace until their bodies give out."

I had to get my English homework from Troy or face Mr. Lanfelt's legendary morning temper. There were still a couple of minutes before class started. Troy was in social studies with Miss DeGracia, so I ran to her class. I caught Troy as he was about to go inside.

"Hey, Troy! I must have given you my English paper by accident."

Troy looked confused. "I already gave everyone their essays," he said. "I didn't see an extra paper, A." He rummaged through his backpack to see if it was there. Then it struck me. When I'd grabbed the papers from the kitchen counter, I could have missed it in my rush to leave.

"Tell you what," Troy said, "I'll ask around. Maybe one of the guys got it, okay?"

I nodded and ran back to English class. When I arrived, everyone was already seated, and Mr. Lanfelt was ambling down the rows of students, collecting assignments. I tried to sneak in quietly but felt his gaze sear me. Sliding into a seat, I tried to clear my mind and defuse my panic. I was just a few minutes late, and Mr. Lanfelt was just a teacher. There was nothing he could do to me, and I had no reason to be afraid of him. Yet I was quivering like a leaf in a winter storm.

"Mr. Lanfelt, I'm sorry—" I started to say, but he cut me off with a sharp look.

"Miss Lee, why don't you tell us who authored that quote on the board?" he demanded.

I looked at the scribbled sentence on the whiteboard:

"TWENTY YEARS FROM NOW YOU WILL BE MORE DISAPPOINTED BY THE THINGS YOU DIDN'T DO THAN BY THE ONES YOU DID!"

Relief flooded in because I knew that quote like the back of my hand. I was about to answer when Mr. Lanfelt turned his disapproving gaze back on me. "Your assignment, Miss Lee?"

I felt my heart beating out of my chest. Today was supposed to be a new beginning, and here I was without my English paper and with a super-lame explanation.

"I don't have it here," I said. "I'll give it to you tomorrow if that's okay."

"Why should you have until tomorrow when everyone else got theirs in on time?" He waited for me to respond, but my tongue twisted. "Answer me, Miss Lee," he insisted. "I'm curious as to what sets you apart from all these other students."

"Listen, the paper is done," I pleaded. "I just can't find it right now."

The other students cast sympathetic glances at me. You could hear a pin drop as Mr. Lanfelt moved down the row.

"So, Miss Lee," he continued, "I take it you're unfamiliar with that quote on the board. Anyone else?"

Yeah, I knew the quote. But at that point I just wanted to disappear and not make things worse. I tried the deep-breaths exercise again, but it wasn't working. Maybe because every time I put out one fire, ten more started up. I shook my head, realizing I was torpedoing down self-pity road. That wasn't good. I had to fight the urge to fall victim to every little problem in my life. Jake's attitude on the subject was summarized by another quote painted on his bedroom wall:

> "HARDSHIPS PREPARE ORDINARY PEOPLE FOR AN EXTRAORDINARY DESTINY."
> C. S. LEWIS

I was alive and healthy, with a good brain that was wide open for business. Nothing stood in my way except me. As long as Jake's voice stayed with me, things would be cool. Or so I kept telling myself.

CHAPTER 9

The low-key rumbling from my classmates brought me back. Someone secretly used their phone to find the answer to Mr. Lanfelt's question. "Mark Twain!" Carter yelled and high-fived a friend. Other students nodded approvingly.

Mr. Lanfelt marched to the front of the room, threw the stack of papers on his desk, and faced the class with a frosty glare. "Does everyone agree with that answer?" he asked.

The class mumbled their endorsement. Who could doubt information splashed all over the internet? The rebel in me battled with my good sense, and it was clear which one was winning. I didn't bother to put up my hand.

"The quote is attributed to Mark Twain," I heard myself say, "but he didn't write it. It's from a book by H. Jackson Brown called *P.S. I Love You.*"

Everyone waited for Mr. Lanfelt to snap some snark back at me, but he didn't. "That's correct, Miss Lee," he said. "Do you know how the rest of the quote goes?"

"I think so," I said.

"Then why don't you finish it on the whiteboard, please."

I got up and approached the front on wobbly legs. Mr. Lanfelt held out a marker, the slight tremor in his hand visible. I tried to smile as I took it, but the corners of my mouth wouldn't move. Once I started writing, I couldn't write fast enough:

"SO THROW OFF THE BOWLINES. SAIL AWAY FROM THE SAFE HARBOR. CATCH THE TRADE WINDS IN YOUR SAILS. EXPLORE. DREAM. DISCOVER."

The words poured out of me because they were very familiar. Jake painted that one above his desk. I never told him Mark Twain didn't write it. I found out by accident while surfing the net for more quotes. It didn't matter who'd written it anyway; it was about what it meant to Jake. And now to me.

I finished writing on the board and walked back to my desk. A couple of students low-fived me as I passed. Mr. Lanfelt remained expressionless. He fanned through the stack of assignment papers, picked one, and faced the class.

"Mr. Ross, would you please do us the honor."

Mr. Lanfelt had found his next victim to humiliate, and I was off the hook for the moment. When the bell rang, everyone packed up and bolted. I couldn't get out of there fast enough, but I'd barely reached the door when Mr. Lanfelt called me back.

"A word, Miss Lee."

I turned reluctantly, expecting him to lash out. He waited until the classroom was clear except for the two of us. Then he wiped the quote off the whiteboard like he was making a point by erasing the words I'd written.

"In case you were wondering," he said, "I think disregarding a paper that counts toward your grade is bold. Reckless, but bold."

"Mr. Lanfelt, like I said, it was an honest mistake. I'll find it and bring it to you."

"If you want a grade on that paper, I get it today," he said. "I'll expect you here at noon to finish it."

"We have a class trip at noon," I said.

"Then the choice is yours. I suggest you choose wisely."

"Why won't you believe me?" I asked. "The paper is done. I just don't have it with me."

"If you're not here precisely at noon, you will get an F for that assignment. And trust me, after your poor performance over the last two months, you cannot afford an F if you want to pass this grade."

Anger ignited frustration. I tried to look at the situation from every angle. Maybe Mr. Lanfelt had had his fill of my slacking off the last two months, sure. And he couldn't know that I'd decided this very morning to turn over a new leaf. On the other hand, why did I get this weird feeling that none of this had anything to do with my paper and everything to do with Mr. Lanfelt picking me to be his emotional punching bag today?

"Responsibility is not an option in life, Miss Lee," he said finally. "It's a reality. See you at noon."

He waved his hand, dismissing me. But the anger dug its claws in deeper and wouldn't let go. Something snapped inside me, and before I knew it, the fury burst out like a fireball.

"Don't talk to me about responsibility," I yelled at him. "I'm not the one who needs to push kids around to feel better about myself. I'm not the one stuck in a life where that first sip of booze is the highlight of my day. I'm not the one who goes home every night with the goal of getting drunk until I pass out. Or who teaches kids every day while battling a hangover. You know, kids who look up to you think that if you can drink with zero consequences, so can they."

As soon as I said all of that, my blood ran cold. I sounded like Mom when she used to yell at Dad. It was the same impulse, every word spiked with hate. But even knowing how much I'd overstepped, I knew there was no turning back. I felt my cheeks flush, the anger still simmering. There was no telling what Mr. Lanfelt would do next, but he was white in the face.

The silence was crushed when Troy burst through the door with a paper in his hand. "Here you are, A!" he said. "Found your paper. It was stuck to one of the others."

He handed it to me, then noticed Mr. Lanfelt. "Oh, hi, teach, what's up? Just bringing Anela's homework to her. Hope it's not too late."

You could have cut the tension in that room with a knife. Troy looked from me to Mr. Lanfelt and backed out with a quick wave.

When Mr. Lanfelt and I were alone again, some color returned to his cheeks.

"That was wrong of me to say," I said. "I'm sorry." My words sounded hollow, tumbling around like they had no substance to them.

Mr. Lanfelt took the paper from my hand and started to read it. My next class was social studies with Miss DeGracia. She'd understand if I explained why I was a little late, but it looked like Mr. Lanfelt was going to finish reading that paper right then and there, no matter how long it took. My insecurities kicked in. Should I have approached the paper's topic differently? Did I check for spelling and grammar?

Then Mr. Lanfelt read out loud from the part where I quoted Shakespeare's *Hamlet*, Act II, scene 2: "What a piece of work is a man, how noble in reason, how infinite in faculty, in form and moving how express and admirable, in action how like an angel, in apprehension how like a god, the beauty of the world, the paragon of animals! And yet to me, what is this quintessence of dust?"

Hearing Mr. Lanfelt speak the King's English and recite Shakespeare's words so perfectly was something else. Finally, he looked up and stared me down for a good twenty seconds. "So, Miss Lee, you agree with Hamlet that the existence of human beings is pointless?" he asked.

That was so unexpected that I had to switch gears in my head. Mr. Lanfelt was asking me to philosophize about the intentions of a writer who'd been dead for four hundred years. But I felt up to the task.

"No, I think we should never stop asking questions about the point of human existence," I said. "We can never take for granted that just because humans act like angels or claim they're noble, they really are. At least I think that's what Shakespeare meant."

"You realize this is English and not social studies, right?" he asked.

"You mean I went all Plato on Shakespeare?" I replied.

"You did indeed, Miss Lee," he said with what looked like a little smile. "Which begs the question: why haven't you entered any of the essay competitions out there? Some of them could help you get into college. You do want to go to college, correct?"

I nodded. Of course I wanted to go to college. But the only way to do that was to get a scholarship. Could that be as easy as writing an essay?

It was common knowledge that Brooklyn High had a history of students winning national essay competitions. Those kids were the go-getters and the brainiacs who made up the debate teams. But they were far removed from the world I lived in.

"I never really thought about it," I lied. I'd given it plenty of thought; I just didn't think I had what it took.

"You should give it some consideration. There is one specific competition that could open the world to you. Pay attention to the bulletin board in the next day or two. That's all, Miss Lee. Tell Miss DeGracia I apologize for making you late."

"Sure," I said quickly.

I would have preferred a verbal whipping after the things I said to him, because this left me confused. *Are we pretending it never happened? Should I apologize again, or what?* He turned his back to me and started writing another quote on the board.

"I didn't mean to be so rude earlier," I said, unsure where I was going with that. "I spoke out of turn, and I shouldn't have—"

"You're going to be very late for your next class, Miss Lee," he interrupted, signaling the end of our discussion. I made my exit with a half-audible "Thanks" and sprinted to Miss DeGracia's class. My head was swirling about the essay competition. Maybe I was really good at writing five-hundred-word essays for other students, but essay competitions were in a class of their own. The self-doubt was already pushing down my enthusiasm. *Am I good enough to enter? Could I deal with it if I lost?*

As I ran down the hall, I glimpsed Shiloh walking across the schoolyard in the distance. The now-familiar flutter in my stomach started up every time I saw or even thought of him. Seeing his vulnerable side today had deepened rather than lessened my feelings for him. He was always so self-assured and in control—or seemed to be. Knowing he battled his own issues somehow made me care even more.

• • •

The next few hours dragged on, until the trip group met in the cafeteria. We got our snack packs and waited for the bus to take us to the State House. There were only about twenty kids in the group. I knew most of them, but they didn't draw me into their cliques. I had it coming after shunning their attention for the past two months.

We piled onto the bus. I had the last few pages of *I Am Malala* to finish, and the forty-five-minute bus trip gave me plenty of downtime. Miss DeGracia walked the aisle and stopped beside me.

"How can you read with all this noise around you?" she asked. "I mean, I envy you for being able to do that."

It took me a few seconds to figure out what she was talking about, but then I heard it too. All around me, kids were talking loudly, playing video games on their phones, and a group of girls was watching *The Bachelor* on an iPad. How did I explain to Miss DeGracia that this kind of racket was nothing new to me? I learned early on to tune out completely. Jake had me do this little exercise where I blocked off my mind, basically creating my own white noise so all that mattered was what I wanted to take in. Sometimes at home, the noise from outside got so loud that I blasted music into my ears to drown it out. Compared to that, the noise on the bus was easy to ignore.

"I'm just about done with *I Am Malala*," I said. "It's a pretty intense read. It makes me realize I have a lot to be thankful for."

"I knew you'd appreciate it," Miss DeGracia said. "My dad always told me, whatever you're going through, there's someone in the world who has it tougher."

Miss DeGracia didn't have a clue about my particular circumstances, only that we lived in a less-fortunate part of the school district. For a second I wanted to ask her what to do about my mom. But I stopped myself from going there. Even if Miss DeGracia liked me, she'd be obligated to report things like that. I couldn't put her under that kind of pressure. And I definitely didn't want to deal with the consequences. So I smiled and nodded like all was right with the world.

"I was really worried about you for a while, Anela," she added. "Jake's death was a terrible loss to us all. I can't imagine how terrifying and painful it had to be for you. I'm happy to see the Anela we all love coming back. I know I've said this before, but if ever you want to talk to someone about it, I'm here for you."

Tears sprang to my eyes, and I looked down to hide them. Miss DeGracia's friendship was like a balm for my soul. A few months ago, I had mentioned to Jake that it would have been wonderful to have someone like Miss DeGracia as a mom.

Jake smiled but shook his head in disagreement. "You don't mean that, A," he said. "Everything that happens in your life has a purpose. Every obstacle in your path is put there to make you stronger. If you had Miss DeGracia for a mom, you might have had more love, but you might also have less of the fight you need inside to rise to the top."

"But I don't feel like I'm rising at all," I complained. "Most of the time I feel stuck."

"That's because you let the noise filter in," Jake said. "You listen to the voices telling you that you can't do something or be something. Only you can decide your path, and you're the only one with the power to shut those voices down."

I turned off the tears and glanced up at Miss DeGracia.

"Thanks, I appreciate it," I said. "That means a lot to me."

She smiled and returned to her seat next to Mr. Rhodes, the other teacher supervising our class trip. Later, I looked out the window and watched the golden dome of the State House come into view. I felt the excitement you feel when something big is about to happen.

CHAPTER 10

I hung back from the rest of the class so I would be the last to enter the senate chamber's second floor, which formed a running balcony above and around the first floor. The room seemed like something from another time. Blue with white trim, it was two stories high, not counting the massive dome that probably doubled the room's height. It looked like a town square, except for the furniture.

The first floor had two colossal, curved tables that formed a circle with short openings on two sides. There must have been forty chairs, at least half filled with state senators. A long, straight desk sat just inside the circle, seating five more. Alcoves holding busts of important people lined the walls, and a giant chandelier hung over everything.

The fluted columns on the second floor made me think of ancient Rome. I could see everything from up there, like an emperor at the Coliseum. But instead of observing gladiators doing battle, I was watching senators argue over a bill.

My heart pounded as I marveled that people's lives changed because of bills passed or rejected right here. The other kids were already goofing around, probably because no phones were allowed. Miss DeGracia had to shush the students more than once. I stood separate from the group because I wanted to take it all in without interruption. Miss DeGracia gave me an encouraging wink.

On the floor below, a female senator finished introducing a new bill. She was Asian and small in stature, but her attitude stood tall. "... is a modest proposal with potentially enormous social benefits, all for the price of a few statewide after-school programs," she concluded.

A heavyset male senator shuffled some papers and peered at her over his glasses.

"Well, Senator Strasberg," he said, "why should we pay to amuse people's kids after school? That's the parents' job."

"So by 'we,'" Strasberg replied, "you mean the parents whose kids will benefit from this program? Because it doesn't come out of your pocket, Senator Linden."

"Not everyone has kids."

"That's true," Strasberg said. "It's also true that not everyone has grandparents with medical conditions. Does that mean we shouldn't help with medical costs?"

"Well—"

"Times are hard. Many households need both parents or the only parent working just to pay the bills, so there's no one at home when school lets out. Do we want vulnerable children wandering the streets, perhaps getting involved with gangs or falling prey to other dangers? Or do we want them in a safe environment with adult supervision? We can make a difference in these children's lives with just a few hours of after-school programs. We have to decide who we are as a society. Do we protect the most vulnerable among us, or do we cast them aside for the sake of a few dollars?"

Linden paused before answering. I leaned forward.

"You make good points, Miss Strasberg," he said, "as always. But this is not an inexpensive program. We cannot allow ourselves to be swayed by emotion."

Strasberg smiled. "No, it's not inexpensive. Nor is your proposed bailout of a certain local industry that's circling the drain because of its own incompetence—and which just so happens to be a substantial contributor to your reelection campaign. But you have no problem bringing that bill to the floor. Is that the headline you want to see? 'State Senator Linden bails out contributors, puts children on the street'?"

Linden frowned, thinking things over, then looked back to his papers.

"Fine," he said at last. "I have no objection to this bill."

I wanted to cheer for Senator Strasberg, but obviously this wasn't a show, and cheering would probably get me thrown out. No one else in the class seemed as impressed as I was. One thing I was sure of: someday, I wanted to do what Senator Strasberg had just done—make a difference in people's lives. Have a hand in making the world a better place for human beings.

A surge of adrenaline hit my body. This was not a common path for someone with my background. It felt so big and out of reach. But I'd find a way.

The senators below us adjourned for the day. The next thing on our schedule was a tour of the State House. I caught up with Miss DeGracia somewhere in the middle of the group and tapped her arm.

"Can I talk to you for a sec, please?" I asked.

"Of course," she said. We stepped to one side, the group filing past us. "That's a pretty big smile on your face, Anela. What's going on?"

"Remember yesterday when you asked if I had any idea what I wanted to do with my future?" I said.

"Yes, I do."

"Promise me you won't laugh?"

"Anela, just tell me!" she said, regarding me earnestly.

"I think I want to become a senator one day. You know, work on making people's lives better. Make the world a better place. Or at least the state."

Miss DeGracia was silent, like she wanted to take care with her response. I immediately assumed she'd say I was reaching too far.

"Okay, give me a second," she said. She took out her phone and texted someone. I was confused but thought maybe she had other business to take care of, so I waited. Her phone dinged, and she turned to me with a grin. "There's someone I want you to meet," she said. "Let me tell Mr. Rhodes that you and I are taking a little side trip."

What does that mean? I wondered. Miss DeGracia looked stoked about something, and I was fine going along for the ride. We strode down long corridors lined with offices.

"Do you remember Senator Strasberg?" she asked. "The one who presented the bill?"

"Yeah," I said. "She's amazing. Watching her made me realize that's what I want to do one day."

"Well, you're about to meet her," Miss DeGracia said. "You can ask her anything you want to know about becoming a senator."

"Are you serious right now?!" I whisper-yelled. "How did you make that happen?"

"We go way back. Senator Strasberg was my mentor at Harvard when she was still teaching there."

"Oh, wow. I should have dressed a little better." I nervously straightened out my coat.

Miss DeGracia laughed. "You look fine. Besides, this is one place where you're judged not by how you dress but by your heart and mind. And, of course, your politics."

We stopped before a door with the nameplate SEN. NASTASIA YEN STRASBERG. I was curious about the combination. Her middle and last names didn't add up.

"She looked Asian to me," I said, "but she has a German last name. Is that her married name?"

"No, Yen is Vietnamese," Miss DeGracia explained. "She was adopted as a little girl. The family was Jewish but decided to keep the first name she was born with."

"She was born in Vietnam?" I asked.

"When we're done here," Miss DeGracia said, "I'll tell you the story of Nastasia Yen Strasberg. It's quite extraordinary."

Miss DeGracia knocked on the door. A young, clean-cut guy in a suit opened it. He was Senator Strasberg's assistant and took us to her office.

"She'll be with you in a minute," he said, leaving us alone.

Senator Strasberg's office was small and cluttered, with books stacked against the walls. It looked like a working office where serious business was conducted. In awe, I didn't know where to look first.

One wall was lined with paintings of American presidents. Another was covered with past and current female world leaders.

"Her office here is exactly the same as it was at Harvard," Miss DeGracia reminisced. "You're looking at a lot of history."

I noticed a small, framed picture on the senator's desk. It was a black-and-white photo of a Vietnamese family: a mom, dad, and two little girls. I took one of the girls to be Senator Strasberg. I couldn't wait to hear the story Miss DeGracia had promised to tell me.

"Eva!" Senator Strasberg said as she walked in. She hugged Miss DeGracia warmly and thrust a hand toward me. "And you must be the young lady who finds this boring place so exciting," she said by way of greeting. I shook her hand like Jake taught me: firm grip, confident shake.

"I'm Anela Lee," I said. "I'm pleased to meet you, Senator."

I glanced at Miss DeGracia to see if I was doing okay. She gave me the tiniest of nods, and I felt encouraged. But the situation was so far removed from my world that I was still nervous.

"Isn't Anela Hawaiian for 'angel'?" Senator Strasberg asked.

"Yes, and it's amazing that you know that," I said.

Senator Strasberg looked at me as though trying to gauge whether she could trust me. She must have decided I wouldn't spill her big secret to the world, because she spoke again in a confidential tone.

"As if I wasn't enough of a nerd as a teen," she said, "my secret hobby was names—their meanings and origins. Back then, you couldn't just Google it. The library was my second home."

"I prefer a library to the web anytime," I said. "My brother and I used to go all the time." Of course, I didn't tell her why Jake and I went to the library or that I hadn't been there since he died. I realized I missed being there and vowed to go again as soon as possible, if for no other reason than to honor Jake's memory.

I looked to Miss DeGracia, and she said, "The first time I met Senator Strasberg, she told me my first name was derived from Hebrew and means 'giver of life.'"

"With a name like that, you should have like six babies," I quipped. A devastated look came over Miss DeGracia. Senator Strasberg put a hand on her arm as if to comfort her. I had said the wrong thing.

But Senator Strasberg had a wonderful social grace and moved on like it never happened. "So," she said, "Eva tells me you're interested in becoming a senator."

I felt the familiar knot twisting in my stomach. It felt ridiculous to tell this accomplished woman—an actual senator—that I had just decided out of the blue to become a senator. "I know it's a long shot," I said. "It was so exciting seeing you fight for a cause and actually get a bill passed today."

"You must mean the after-school programs bill. It's not passed yet, but the chances are good. I've lost plenty of fights, too. It's not always easy. But let's get back to this long-shot thing. Why in the world would you think that?"

Embarrassment heated my cheeks. *How can I explain it to her?* But she didn't wait for me to make excuses. Her gaze drifted to the images of American presidents and female leaders.

"Do you think any of them allowed obstacles to stand in their way?" she asked.

All I could do was shrug. How could she compare my struggles to those of American presidents? Our backgrounds were nothing alike.

"I can't relate to old White men," I said. "I'm sorry."

Senator Strasberg's gentle demeanor didn't mask her strength, and I could see how she convinced others to pass her bills.

"Humans all bleed the same color," she said. "We have the same basic needs in life. And when those needs are jeopardized, we react in different ways. These are the people I wrote about in my dissertation. Every one of them proves that it doesn't matter where you come from or how tough things might be. You can overcome all of it and still achieve your dream."

"Oh yeah?" I said.

"What, did you think they were all rich kids with perfect families and easy lives?"

"I don't know enough about them," I said. "But they all look like they might have had pretty easy lives."

Miss DeGracia smiled and took a seat, like she knew where things went from here.

Senator Strasberg gestured to a wall displaying twelve pictures of young boys. I had been too distracted to notice them. The photos looked to have been taken between the 1920s and the 1980s. I had no idea who those boys were, but I was pretty sure Senator Strasberg was about to tell me.

CHAPTER 11

"Pick one," Senator Strasberg said. "Anyone."

I pointed to a boy with brown skin, wearing a white shirt. He seemed about ten years old and was standing at an airport, arms crossed over his chest. He looked happy.

"Let's call him Huss for now," Senator Strasberg said. "His mother's name was Stanley. Yes, really. His father's name was Rack. She was from Washington State, and he was from Kenya. They met in Hawaii and fell in love. When Huss was two, his father abandoned the family and moved to Massachusetts, then back to Africa. Huss didn't see him again for eight years. 'After a week of seeing my father in the flesh,' he wrote later, 'I had decided that I preferred his more distant image, an image I could alter on a whim—or ignore when convenient.'"

I thought about that. It was exactly the way I felt about Dad most of the time. As much as I wanted to love him, it was easier to love Dad when he was far away; the reality was complicated. I hardly thought of him anymore because most of the memories weren't good.

The mention of Hawaii clued me in on who the boy might be.

Senator Strasberg gave me a moment to digest that, then continued. "Huss moved to Indonesia for four years, where his mother remarried. His stepfather was good to him, but Indonesia wasn't like America. Scurvy and polio were still problems there.

"One day, a man with no nose came to the house, asking for food. The hole in his face whistled when he spoke. It was common to see people with no arms or feet or with bodies twisted by deformities, all making their way around on homemade carts. That made a monumental impression on Huss, and it followed him for the rest of his life.

"When he finally moved back to Hawaii, he lived with his grandparents because his mother spent a lot of time in Indonesia with her second husband and their daughter."

"What happened to Huss?" I asked, though I was pretty sure I knew.

Strasberg smiled. "I'll give you a hint. His full name is Barack Hussein Obama."

In some ways, his life had been more messed up than mine. I looked closely at the picture, my nose almost touching the glass. Now I saw the resemblance.

"Not what you were expecting?" Strasberg asked.

"Not at all," I said, mesmerized. "He's a cool dude. He makes being a good man look easy." My curiosity sparked now, I wanted to sponge up any information Senator Strasberg was willing to share with me.

I pointed to another picture, this one in black and white. The boy looked pensive, as if he held the world's secrets in his eyes.

Senator Strasberg studied the boy's picture. "That's twelve-year-old Mils," she said. "He was such a talented piano player that his parents thought he might become a famous pianist someday. Mils's family were Quakers, and they lived in Southern California.

"Mils loved his little brother, Arthur, very much, and when Arthur got sick and slipped into a coma, Mils was shattered. He prayed for Arthur to get better, but little Arthur died. His mother, Hannah, wrote that Mils 'was so sad, he was numb with shock and grief.' She said Mils 'sank into a deep, impenetrable silence.' When Mils was in college, he wrote an essay about Arthur, describing his despair. He said that looking at Arthur's picture reminded him of hope."

I felt an instant connection with Mils, and I think Senator Strasberg could see how her stories affected me. "Eight years later, when he was twenty," she said, "Mils's older brother, Harold, also died. Mils's 'fierce determination was intensified' because he was trying to be three sons in one to make up for his parents' loss. His mother said Mils was guilt ridden that Harold and Arthur were dead and he was still alive."

"I think I know who this is," I said. Miss DeGracia and the senator regarded me curiously. "Richard Milhous Nixon."

Senator Strasberg grinned. "That's pretty impressive. Not many people know his story."

"I read an article about him," I told her. "I barely remember the rest of it, but I remember that. The guilt, I mean."

I was about to point to another picture when Senator Strasberg's assistant stuck his head in the door. It felt like I'd been in her office all day instead of just a short while.

"Your next appointment is in three minutes," the assistant said. Senator Strasberg nodded. She probably noticed the disappointment cloaking me from head to toe.

Miss DeGracia stood and gestured at the towers of books stacked on the floor. "Nastasia, don't you need someone to catalog these books and bring some order to the office? Because I know someone who might be willing to help you out."

Senator Strasberg looked my way. "I get the feeling Eva is trying to put you to work."

"Oh, I could totally do that," I said, then worried I sounded overly enthusiastic. I took a deep breath. "I'd love the opportunity to help you out, Senator Strasberg. I can start immediately."

"Well, how about we start on Saturday?" she said. "Weekends are usually a little more peaceful here."

"Saturday is great," I said. "What time?"

"I usually start my day at seven, but I'll ask Daniel to pick you up at eight thirty."

"No, it's fine!" I said, too quickly. "I mean, I can get here by myself."

"Okay, I like that," she said. "Asserting your independence. As long as you know when to accept help."

I didn't mind Senator Strasberg thinking I was independent. The truth was, my neighborhood was embarrassing. But all of that was pushed out of my head by the fact that I was officially going to work for a senator.

After Miss DeGracia and I said our goodbyes to Senator Strasberg, I filled out forms and got my photo taken for a temporary State House identification pass. The whole time, I was wishing Jake could see me. He'd be so proud. He would have taken me to the twelve-dollar Chinese buffet. I pictured myself telling him how weird things had started out this morning and how it all somehow morphed into this fantastic day.

. . .

Miss DeGracia sat beside me on the bus ride back to school.

"Thank you for introducing me to Senator Strasberg," I said. "I can't believe this is happening."

Miss DeGracia laughed. "At Harvard, I organized Nastasia's office library every Friday afternoon. For four years. Those couple of hours a week meant the world to me. She has so much wisdom and a huge heart."

"I said something back there I shouldn't have," I said. "About you having kids. You looked upset. I'm sorry."

"My reaction had nothing to do with you," Miss DeGracia said. "The simple truth is, I can't have kids. It's one of those realities that hits you when you least expect it."

It took me a minute to absorb that someone as kind and loving as Miss DeGracia couldn't have kids, while people like my parents could, without even trying.

"You can always adopt," I suggested. "And it's easier than you think, especially if you're open to adopting any race."

"Of course I'm open to adopting any race. That's not the problem at all. It's because I'm not married. They're not so keen on letting single people adopt babies."

"I didn't know that," I said, and we stared out the window. "What did Senator Strasberg teach at Harvard?" I asked at length. I wanted to conduct some research so I didn't sound like a fool when I talked to my new boss.

"Well, this is where it gets interesting," Miss DeGracia said. "Nastasia has a master's degree in psychology and a master's and PhD in American history. That's why she knows so much about the presidents and what it took for them to succeed. Nastasia is of the opinion that people deal with trauma in different ways. Some allow it to pull them into a dark abyss, while others use it as a building block. Some of the most successful people in the world had to endure severe trauma when they were young."

Senator Strasberg's research backed up what Jake had told me all along. No matter your background, you could reach great heights—and the person responsible for climbing out of the black pit, toward the light, was you. There might be angels along the way, giving you a nudge when you held back or cheering you on as you moved forward. But the real work was up to you.

"Does this have anything to do with her childhood?" I asked. "You said you'd tell me her story."

"Okay, but I have to warn you, it's pretty sad."

I nodded. My curiosity about what made Nastasia Strasberg tick far outweighed my fear of feeling sad.

"Nastasia was born in Vietnam during the war. At the end, American soldiers were trying to evacuate thousands of people from Saigon. It was called Operation Frequent Wind. People were told to go to the US embassy for evacuation. Nastasia was two at the time. She went there with her parents and younger sister."

A chill ran down my back. "Did they all make it out?"

"It wasn't that easy," Miss DeGracia said. "Everyone was trying to get into the embassy because they could see helicopters coming and going, taking people to US Navy ships off the coast. People came from all over the city, trying to push through the gates or climb the wall.

"As the North Vietnamese army got closer, President Ford ordered the helicopters to evacuate the remaining Americans from the embassy compound. So they did, and everyone else was left behind. Nastasia's family didn't even make it through the gate. She remembers them turning away as the last helicopters left."

"How did they get out then?" I asked. I was almost afraid to hear the answer.

"When President Ford wouldn't send the helicopters back for refugees, the US ambassador convinced the Navy to keep the fleet off the coast for a few more days in case anyone else managed to escape. Some came in boats, some in South Vietnamese helicopters. Because the pilots weren't going back, the Americans pushed the empty helicopters into the ocean to make room for new arrivals."

"That's pretty drastic," I said.

"They did what they had to do. Nastasia's father spent the last of his money to get the family on a boat, but by the time they reached the Navy ships, they were already full. Nastasia's parents somehow convinced soldiers to take their two small daughters on board. Nastasia remembers 'rising into the sky' beside her sister, her parents getting smaller below her as she was pulled up by rope. It's her last memory of that day."

Miss DeGracia gazed out the window for a moment. The people going about their day, living their lives, provided a stark contrast to the story she was telling me.

"There weren't many records from the ship," she said. "Just bits and pieces of information from other passengers that Nastasia put together with partial memories to find out what happened."

"I can't even imagine the panic the little girls must have felt," I said.

"Nastasia never saw her parents again. I'm pretty sure they would have come looking for their daughters if they had survived the war."

"What about her sister?" I asked. Anxiety for the little girls filled my whole being.

"Nastasia and her little sister were separated on the ship. Nastasia never saw her again, either. Everyone was dropped off in the Philippines. From there, most of them were shipped to America. There was no record of Nastasia's Vietnamese family name. Just the photo her parents must have put in her pocket."

That had to be the most tragic and unusual history for any US politician. I tried to imagine what it would be like to grow up with a past like that.

"Has Senator Strasberg tried to find her family again?" I asked.

"She tried for about ten years, back in the eighties," Miss DeGracia said. "But she gave up because there wasn't enough information to follow up on. Things were so chaotic in Saigon that parents were scribbling family names on their children. Some didn't even get a chance to do that. Nastasia was too young to know her last name. She only knew that her Vietnamese name was Yen."

"And then she was adopted here?"

"By the Strasberg family, yes," Miss DeGracia said. "They were Jewish, so she was raised in that religious tradition. She counts herself fortunate to have been part of such a loving family. The one thing that still haunts her is not knowing what happened to her sister."

CHAPTER 12

I thought about Senator Strasberg's story as I set out for Tamara's house. There was a lot of time to think; few buses ran through Tamara's neighborhood, and the schedules didn't line up.

To be separated from family at such a young age and then taken to a country where everyone looked and spoke differently must have been awful. Miss DeGracia said the family photo had run in a few American and Vietnamese newspapers, but no one recognized Strasberg's parents. Strasberg had stopped looking after that because her efforts always ended in disappointment.

To the rest of the world, Nastasia Strasberg had been a happy, well-adjusted teenager, then a Harvard scholar and state senator. I concluded that a traumatic past pushed some people to succeed while filling others with doubts and insecurities. It was time to face reality. I had the tools and the opportunity to make something of my life; the only thing holding me back was me. The mind was a powerful thing. I just needed to learn how to control it. But I also wondered if there was more to it than that.

When the bus finally dropped me near Tamara's neighborhood, I had another mile to walk. I hoped Shiloh wasn't home. The last thing I needed was him seeing the sweaty mess I would be by the time I got there.

I was walking along, minding my own business, when a cop car rolled slowly past. I tried to ignore the inquisitive stare, but it stung anyway. It made me feel guilty, even when I wasn't doing anything wrong. The fire in my belly ignited. I wanted to yell that I was visiting a friend and had every right to be where I was. But I could hear Jake telling me to ease back and take a deep breath. Some police officers might choose to interpret standing up for myself as anger or resistance. And Jake knew how that went.

On Christmas Eve four years ago, we woke up to someone banging on the front door and screaming, "Police! Open up!"

I heard Jake run past my bedroom toward the front door. Two seconds later, the cops were yelling so loud that it sounded like they were right next to me, even with my bedroom door closed. I went to look, and my stomach dropped. Two cops were pressing Jake's face against the wall and handcuffing him. I saw the vein in Jake's neck swelling with anger, but he stayed calm.

"You have the wrong apartment, sir," he said. "You have the wrong person."

That made one of the cops mad, and he got pretty rough with Jake. I started crying, and as the second cop pushed me back, the angry cop slammed my brother's face into the wall.

"Stay here! Stay here!" the second cop yelled at me. "Or you get arrested too."

I was a skinny eleven-year-old and hardly a threat to two big men. Petrified and confused, I just wanted to help my brother.

"Where's your mom?" the second cop asked me.

"She's working night shift," I cried.

"Where's your dad?"

"I don't know!" I yelled. "What are you doing to Jake? Why are you hurting him?"

I tried to move past the cop, but he wouldn't let me. A steady stream of blood ran from Jake's nose. I was furious by now, but I knew Jake would want me to stay calm like he was.

The lights of our small Christmas tree flickered in the living room behind the intruders—Jake's attempt to make Christmas special for me. A few small gifts sat under the tree. Some had little cards that said they were to me from Mom and Dad, but I knew Jake bought all of them. Every Christmas Day, Jake would make the whole family watch *Miracle on 34th Street*. We'd start early, before Dad passed out from drinking too much. Mom even cooked a nice dinner once or twice.

Once upon a time I had told Jake to stop going to the trouble because it seemed to cause more issues between Mom and Dad. The next year, Jake set the little Christmas tree up in my room, and the two of us went to Beacon's Diner a few blocks away, where they served Christmas dinners on the cheap. But even that caused turmoil at home since Mom and Dad preferred an unhappy family together over half the family away and happy. The year after that, we were back to a tree in the living room.

A third cop barged into our tiny apartment. The angry cop looked ready to explode. The newcomer screamed at the first two cops that they had the wrong apartment and the wrong person. The cop in front of me stepped aside, but the angry cop kept holding Jake hostage, pressing his face into the wall and yelling at him. The other two cops had to pull him away.

A minute later, it was over, the cops storming out with no apology. Jake sank to the floor, bleeding and in tears. I swallowed my panic and held him until he stopped shaking. For once, I was the strong one, and I wanted to push that strength into Jake. I told him it was safe now and that everything would be okay, though I didn't believe it myself. I wiped the blood from his face. A minute later we heard the cops yelling outside, followed by gunshots. I wanted to run to the window and see what was going on, but Jake pulled me back.

"You don't need to see any of that," he said. It was the only time I ever heard rage crackling in Jake's throat. "But let me tell you now," he warned, "whatever you believe the truth is, never fight the cops. Just do what they tell you. For some cops, the color of your skin is reason enough to abuse you. Or worse."

"How is that fair?" I said.

"It's not fair, Anela. None of it's fair. We just gotta find a way out of this place. It's that simple." I jumped when we heard someone falling against the front door, but Jake didn't flinch. "It's probably

Dad," he said. "Go to bed. I'll get him inside."

"No, I'll help you," I said. "Stop taking all of this on your shoulders, Jake. I'm eleven. It's time we worked together."

Jake patted my head. "You're really some kinda special, A."

We opened the front door, and sure enough, Dad was passed out in the hallway. He was a big man, and dragging him inside would take a lot of effort.

Jake slapped Dad's face. "Hey, you gotta get inside," he said. "Come on. Get up."

But Dad was in no shape to stand, let alone walk. He mumbled something incoherent and started snoring. Jake waved me inside the apartment.

"Let's leave him," he said. "This is on him, not us."

"How's leaving him in the hallway not looking for more trouble tonight?" I asked. "The place is crawling with cops."

Jake shook his head and reluctantly lingered in the doorway.

"You take one arm. I'll get the other," I said, leaving no doubt that this was happening, even if I had to do it myself. Jake sighed, and together we dragged Dad inside and planted him on the ratty couch. Jake did most of the work, but I can't say he was gentle. He was still angry and now felt free to express his internal rage.

"What kind of father are you?" he yelled into Dad's unconscious face. "What kind of father does this to his kids?"

Dad's eyes slit open for a split second like he was deciding how to answer the question. But then his eyelids fell shut, saving him the trouble.

Outside, cop cars and an ambulance crowded the street. Red and blue lights danced on the windows, casting crazy shadows on the walls. I removed Dad's shoes and placed them neatly side by side. Then I draped a blanket over his bulky form. Jake watched me with a mixture of impatience and love.

"You have school in the morning," he said. "Let's get you to bed."

Once Jake made sure I was in bed and covered up, he hung a

blanket over the window to muffle the sounds outside and keep them from entering my dreams.

• • •

Tamara's house was still a ways off, and it was getting dark. I walked a little faster, trying to seem as if I belonged here and knew where I was going. When the cop car slowed even more—so much that I caught up with it—my aggravation doubled, and my face got hot.

"What do you want?" I yelled, then immediately regretted it. I'd promised Jake I'd avoid trouble when I could. Now that promise was broken into a thousand pieces.

The cop car stopped. My heart hammered in my throat when the cop got out, but I waited. There was no undoing things now. The cop left his door open, and sounds of the radio drifted out. As he came closer, fear took hold of me and wouldn't let go.

"I'm sorry," I said. "I didn't mean to yell at you."

The cop slowed his pace, then stopped. "Easy now. It's okay," he said. "Just want to know you're safe. I always check on kids walking alone when it gets dark."

I hadn't seen that coming, so I just stood there with a mouth full of teeth and nothing to say.

"Kid, you're worrying me now. Are you okay?"

I nodded. "Sure, I'm just going to my friend's house," I said. "They don't run too many buses around here."

"I hear you," he said with a comforting smile. "When I started patrolling here, that's the first thing I noticed. How far do you have to go?"

"It's only a few blocks now," I said.

He started back to his patrol car. "Tell you what: hop in, and I'll get you there faster. Safest ride in town."

It was a short trip, but we talked a little. He introduced himself as Dave Dunster and asked me how the rest of my day had been. I was astounded that this strange person, a cop no less, made me feel comfortable enough to share, and the words came tumbling out. He listened until I was done telling him about the State House and meeting Senator Strasberg.

"Hold on," he said. "All that happened today?"

I smiled. "I know, right? I wouldn't believe it if it hadn't happened to me."

"You'd better believe it," he said. "You just keep making those waves, okay?"

When we stopped in front of Tamara's gigantic home, he shook my hand. "I'll remember your name. The day you're up for election, I'll throw my vote your way."

I laughed. "That's still a ways off, but thanks. And thanks for the ride. You're a good man."

"Just trying to stay in a future senator's good books," he said, waving as he drove off. I didn't expect to see Dave Dunster again, but he left an indelible impression. My first potential constituent. It felt good.

CHAPTER 13

I was texting Tamara that I was outside when the front door swung open and her dad stormed out, almost running me over. He had an ugly look on his face.

"Hi," I managed to say, then jumped out of the way.

"Oh, it's you again," he said, then got in his shiny Range Rover and slammed the door. *What is it about me that aggravates him so much?* I wondered. He knew nothing about me. Again I heard Jake's words: "You can never force a person to respect you, A. But you can refuse to be disrespected."

"How do you refuse to be disrespected?" I'd asked. "That doesn't make sense."

"By washing it off like dirt from your hands," Jake said. "People who disrespect others crave the reaction. They live to hurt people. By refusing to let it get to you, you deny them the satisfaction."

I looked at Tamara's dad as he sat in the Range Rover, staring me down with disdain on his face. I smiled and forced a friendly little wave. His failure to intimidate me clearly left him annoyed, because he gunned the Range Rover from the driveway, tires screeching. *Maybe he'll speed past the cop and get caught.* I immediately expelled that idea from my mind. It was not my place to wish revenge on someone I didn't know.

In my brief time in Senator Strasberg's office, I'd learned that you couldn't read anyone from outside appearances alone. Everyone faced challenges, but not everyone was equipped to handle them gracefully. Who knew how much of a mess I might have been if not for Jake? It was like he'd been put on this earth to be my guardian angel and guide me safely through our stormy home life. I suddenly found myself empathizing with Tamara and Shiloh's dad. Maybe he'd had no one in his life to guide him. Maybe he was alone in fighting the rage inside him. Tamara told me once that her dad's childhood was abusive. His ongoing anger had to stem from that. I quietly vowed to always be nice to him, regardless of how he treated me.

Tamara's mom, Isabel, opened the front door and let me inside. Predictably, she went into rescue mode. "You must be freezing, Anela," she said. "Come in. Let's get you a warmer winter coat. Tamara has so many she won't miss one or two."

I thought back to one of our sleepovers. When school let out that day, dozens of high-end SUVs lined the street, waiting to pick up the rich kids. Tamara and I headed for her mom's Porsche.

"Just tell her we can go to the mall another day, okay?" I said to Tamara. Her mom was very sweet, but apparently it took a daily handful of prescription pills to maintain that state of angelic oblivion.

Tamara shrugged. "Fine, but it's really confusing why you wouldn't milk the situation for all it's worth. So she wants to buy you stuff. So what?"

"I'm not a charity case—that's all," I said.

We climbed into the back seat, and Isabel's breathless voice dominated everything.

"Hi, Anela!" she said a little too enthusiastically. "I'm taking you girls to the mall. We're going to do some shopping today. A new shop opened up right next to the Louis Vuitton store."

I shot Tamara a questioning look. She giggled and shrugged back helplessly. Once at the mall, we basically followed Isabel around as she hopped from one clothing store to the next, picking out stuff she thought Tamara or I would look pretty in. I wanted to put a stop to it, but Tamara cornered me in a dressing room.

"Just let her do this," she whispered. "It puts her in a good mood when she thinks she's doing something special for someone else."

So I tagged along, nodded, modeled, and smiled. Inside, I cringed at the notion that I was responsible for making a rich lady feel good about herself. I texted that to Jake. He sent back five laughing emojis and said: "Run with it, A. Think of it as your good points for the week."

Later that night, Tamara and I tried all the clothes on again. When I put on the yellow dress, Tamara clapped her hands.

"You look so beautiful!" she said.

But I didn't like what I saw in the mirror. A completely different person stared back at me. Someone who was screaming for attention. I preferred to keep things on the down-low and disappear in the crowd. It felt safer that way.

I shared my thoughts with Tamara as gently as I could.

"Between us," I said, "this just isn't me. I'm more 'understated' than 'in your face.'"

"What about the pink dress?" Tamara asked. "That's not too bright."

I sat on the canopy bed beside her. "I appreciate what your mom is trying to do," I said. "But this is a waste on someone like me. These clothes don't fit my life."

Tamara was unfazed. "So take the clothes back to the shops and keep the money, honey."

Clearly that had been Tamara's plan all along.

"I see what you're doing here," I told her.

Tamara giggled, busted. "Well, you never want to accept help, and it's driving me crazy."

"I really don't need help," I assured her. But I knew it fell on deaf ears. "Besides, I have Jake. We look after each other just fine."

Tamara looked wistful and hesitated before confessing, "You're lucky to have Jake. I almost never see Shiloh. And when I do, it's like we hardly have anything to say to each other."

I felt bad for Tamara and tried to console her.

"He has to be pretty busy," I said, probably unconvincingly. "Being editor of the school newspaper and all that."

"He doesn't feel like a brother," Tamara said. "He feels like a distant relative I see once a week."

"Have you tried talking to him?" I asked.

"It doesn't work like that in this house," Tamara said. "We're four strangers living together. Talking is one thing this family never does."

• • •

Isabel's voice brought me back to the present. "Right this way," she said, leading the way to Tamara's room. I was shocked to see a pale, fragile girl in the bed. I'd been so wrapped up in my grief that I barely paid attention to anything else. But missing Tamara's health going downhill so fast? Guilt consumed me. I sat on the bed, wanting to hug her but afraid I might hurt her.

"Mom, could you give us a minute?" Tamara said. "We just want to catch up on stuff."

"Sure, I'll get Maria to make you some food." Isabel left the room reluctantly. Tamara took my hand, and the words spilled out of her. "You have no idea how great it is to see you," she said. "I tried so many times to text you, but I figured you were never going to text me back. I'm so sorry about Jake." She pulled me in for a hug, and tears stung my eyes.

"And I'm sorry for not paying enough attention to realize you weren't in school for a while," I said. "I saw Shiloh today, and he couldn't tell me anything."

"Shiloh doesn't know the full story. He's so wrapped up in his own little world, performing like a circus monkey, trying to impress Dad. Besides, he thinks there's nothing that modern medicine can't fix."

"Well, what is it you have?" I asked. "You're going to be okay, right?"

"My stupid kidneys decided to get weird on me."

"That could mean anything," I said, worried. "Will it get better?"

"Sure," Tamara replied. "I'm on dialysis now."

"I don't even know what that is."

"It basically does what your kidneys are supposed to do," Tamara said matter-of-factly. "It helps to remove waste, salt, and water to stop them from building up in your body."

"Okay, so is that to give your kidneys a break while they get healthy again?" I asked.

"Yeah, something like that," Tamara said. "But, hey, let's not talk about it. I have so much else to tell you."

Tamara confessed that her comment about her mom never allowing Shiloh to go out with a girl who came from where I did had been made out of jealousy. She was petrified that my interest in Shiloh might take my attention away from my friendship with her.

"I should have figured that out," I said. "And talked to you instead of judging."

"No, you were right to walk away, Anela. What I said was insanely stupid."

"Hey, you said you were sorry," I said. "Not many people are big enough to admit they were wrong. And I don't think you should worry about me and Shiloh ever getting together. He's not interested in me in *that* way."

"Hmm, that's funny," Tamara said with a secretive smile. "Because the only time we talk is when he asks about you." My heart skipped a beat, but I didn't let it go to my head. I doubted a guy like Shiloh would take on a complicated mess like me.

After a bit, Isabel brought some hot chocolate and grilled cheese sandwiches. My stomach rumbled when I smelled the food. We all laughed at the funny noise, and Isabel pushed the tray toward me, encouraging me to eat. I stuffed my face with the sandwich and chugged down the hot chocolate. Money might not be everything, but the food it bought sure tasted good.

Isabel sat on the other side of the bed. "I don't know if Tamara has told you," she said, "but we need someone to help with her schoolwork six hours a week. The teachers have been great sending assignments, but Tamara really needs more help."

"Oh sure, I could totally do that," I said.

"We'll pay you three hundred a week plus expenses, including an Uber back and forth."

I shook my head. "You don't have to pay me. I'd be happy to do it. The Uber would be cool, though. The bus service around here is bad."

"Anela, I'm not taking no for an answer," Isabel said. "And I promise not to take you mall shopping again. I was overstepping, and I shouldn't have."

For the first time, I saw vulnerability in Isabel. Her usual spacey look was gone. Everything she did, or planned to do, was to benefit Tamara. She'd always been a good mom, but now she was a clear-eyed woman who didn't rely on feel-good pills to get her through the day.

"No more mall shopping?" I said. "Then you've got yourself a deal."

Isabel winked at us. "Why don't you girls visit for an hour? Then I'll get an Uber for Anela." She turned to me. "And thank you. I appreciate you being here for Tamara." She left the room and closed the door.

I stared at Tamara. "This is more serious than you're letting on, isn't it?" I asked.

Tamara stalled for time by pushing her untouched plate of food toward me.

"Have mine," she said. "I already had dinner."

"Thanks, but answer my question, please."

"I told you everything I know," she said. "I'm going to get better. And at least we're friends again, and that's literally all that matters to me right now. Why don't you tell me about everything I've missed."

I decided not to tell Tamara about my life-changing day, instead keeping it to small talk about school and mutual acquaintances.

"I heard Monique is having a party on Friday," Tamara said.

"Yeah, she invited me," I confirmed. "It's my first party ever, and I'm not sure if I'm gonna fit into that scene."

"Shiloh's going," Tamara said.

"Oh, I didn't think it would be his thing."

"That's exactly what I told him. He said there's nothing wrong with trying out new experiences. I think he's entered the rebellious-teen stage. Next thing you know, he'll want to play ice hockey."

I couldn't help but smile. "Well, about a million people are going to Monique's party," I said. "I'll be invisible in the crowd."

"Exaggerate much?" Tamara asked. "You're only invisible if you want to be. But at least Shiloh talks to you. Troy never says anything to me other than 'Hi' or 'Yo.'"

"Wouldn't your mom have a problem with you dating him?" I asked carefully.

"This whole at-death's-door thing has changed the way my mom sees a lot of things, believe me."

"Well, like I told you before," I said, "all you have to do is take the leap and ask Troy out."

"Sure," Tamara agreed. "But let me shake this little 'infirmity' first."

I had to laugh. I thought the visit might be tense; it was anything but. We picked up exactly where we left off, and it felt great to have someone to share secrets with again.

Time flew past, and I could see why Tamara's mom only gave us an hour. By the time Isabel knocked on the door, Tamara seemed out of it. We said our goodbyes, and Isabel walked me to the front door, where an Uber was waiting. She hugged me before I left.

"Your friendship is very important to my daughter," she said. "And Tamara is very important to me. If you need anything, just ask."

I left feeling good, even optimistic—though I still didn't know how serious Tamara's illness was. She said something about time and patience, so I had to respect that. If denial was Tamara's coping mechanism, more power to her. There was strength in thinking positive and not feeling sorry for yourself.

I checked my phone in the Uber to see if Mom had messaged. I'd texted her three times during the day, but she still hadn't gotten back to me. When the Uber driver stopped at my apartment building, we saw two men arguing out front.

"It's all good. They're just loudmouths," I told the driver. But she wasn't having any of it. She parked the car and said she wasn't moving until I was safely inside. I walked right past the troublemakers and waved to the driver as I went in.

The apartment hall at night was creepy enough when the lights were working, never mind when they weren't—like now. I wasn't used to braving it alone. Then there was the lingering smell of moldy carpet, worse in winter. And it seemed a little more paint peeled off the walls each year. I held my breath, afraid of inhaling spores or whatever was rotting under the floors and in the walls. Thinking I saw a shadow at the end of the hallway, I unlocked the apartment as fast as I could, slipped inside, and bolted the door.

CHAPTER 14

I was ready to crawl into bed and sleep, but I had homework. There was no sign of Mom in the apartment. I was past worrying about her. My head was filled with so much stuff that I had to pick and choose what to deal with first.

Friday night was the party at Monique's. I was fine with her dressing me up. At least that was one less thing to worry about.

I went to Jake's room to check for what money remained after paying rent. His smell was still everywhere. I expected a cloud of misery to envelop me, but it didn't. That I felt okay was kind of shocking. So, this was the place of peace you reached when the shards of your broken heart came together again. A rush of nostalgia, but without your world coming apart.

The vault produced a ten-dollar bill squished underneath the gun. I stuffed the bill in my pocket. Once again, seeing the gun made me feel unsteady. I needed to get rid of it and decided to speak to Troy. There was no easy way to approach the subject, but if anyone else knew about the gun, it would be Troy.

It was midnight by the time I finished my homework, and there was still no sign of Mom. She hadn't returned my texts, and after seeing how dazed she was this morning, I needed to know she was okay. The only thing left to do was call the care facility where she worked the night shift.

"Is Sophia Lee working tonight?" I asked the man who answered the phone. He sounded half-asleep and in no mood to deal with anyone.

"Sophia don't work here no more," he said. "She was fired a week ago."

My heart sank. "Are you sure?" I asked. But the only answer I got was the beep telling me the call had ended.

My first thought was to wonder how we'd pay the rent. My mind was on overload.

I didn't mind helping out with the bills, but I couldn't carry the brunt by myself. And if Mom wasn't at work, where was she? Dread crept back into my psyche. I contemplated texting Dad, but that would be a wasted effort. First off, he never texted back. Second, he'd be passed out by now. Jake said it wasn't a weakness to ask for help, but I didn't have anyone I could trust. I'd never felt more alone in my life.

I went back to Jake's room, and for a good ten minutes, I gazed at the quotes we'd written on the walls. There was always one that connected me to the moment, but not this time. Maybe I was just tired. Still, it felt like everything would come crashing down like a tidal wave if I didn't find a smidgeon of hope. And I'd be right back where I was before Jake's voice found me after a two-month silence.

A split second before giving up, I found a quote written near the corner of the back wall, right beneath the window. It was scribbled in small script, in Jake's handwriting. Almost as if he wanted me to find it only when I needed it most:

"I DON'T THINK OF THE MISERY,
BUT OF THE BEAUTY THAT STILL REMAINS."

Unlike the other quotes on the walls, this one had no attribution. It seemed familiar. I felt compelled to know who wrote it and under what circumstances. If nothing else, finding out would distract me from my current state of mind.

I Googled the quote. It was by Anne Frank, the fifteen-year-old Jewish girl who hid from the Nazis in World War II. I'd read *The Diary of Anne Frank* for sixth-grade social studies, and it all came back to me. Anne was one of eight people living in a cramped space for two years. That would test most people's tolerance. But where others saw darkness, Anne saw light. Despite her circumstances, she believed there was still hope. And while she was physically unable to go outside, she wrote that no one had the power to confine her mind. Writing was her escape; she described her fears, frustrations, moments of happiness, and the dreams of a girl on the verge of womanhood. She spoke of a mother who didn't understand her, a sister who felt distant. And a boy she didn't love at first but then missed when he wasn't there.

If Anne Frank can have hope when surrounded by misery, who am I to doubt the light at the end of the tunnel? I simply had to look ahead.

I decided to add Anne Frank to the club. It was a thing now. I'd created a folder on my computer, "Anela's Club," filled with stories of people who inspired me. People who, in their darkest hours, still found hope and determination. Senator Strasberg's story was the first I included.

I decided to go to bed. It was cold, and all I wanted to do was crawl under the warm covers and think about how to overcome my problems instead of worrying about them. Of course, my mind didn't work that way. I came up with solutions for trivial stuff but couldn't let go of the thing that bothered me most.

I kept telling myself Mom was at work, and her phone was switched off, or she was too busy to text back. It wasn't like we were used to texting back and forth. Communication had always been minimal; we just said what needed to be said. But today I felt the need to check in on her and make sure she was okay. If she was using drugs, she needed support, not judgment. And the only thing standing in the way of that was the resentment anchored inside me. Pushing my anger aside was way easier said than done.

I allowed the day to wash over me. I remembered how surprised I was when Nastasia Strasberg told me about "Huss" and "Mils." How my impression of American presidents coming from fancy, trouble-free backgrounds had been destroyed. They say never judge a book by its cover, and that couldn't be more appropriate than it was here. Or even with Shiloh. I always thought he had an easy life, but now I felt glad not to be in his shoes.

I thought of Senator Strasberg's journey from Vietnam to America. How many lives were better because of her relentless fight for justice and equality? And probably none of them knew about her long journey to the State House. Jake would have liked her. He would have thought her an honorable human being. It was what he strove for in his own life. And he would have been happy to see her become my mentor.

I decided to do what I could to discover what happened to Nastasia Strasberg's family.

As I fell asleep, I thought about Mr. Lanfelt telling me I should enter essay competitions. I was curious as to why he mentioned that out of the blue. Maybe Miss DeGracia told him I had bigger plans for my life. There were rumors about her and Mr. Lanfelt being an item, but I didn't believe it for a second. She'd never be involved with someone like that. And then I immediately felt guilty for thinking of Mr. Lanfelt as "someone like that."

On the wall above his bed, Jake had painted his favorite quote from the Bible:

"FIRST TAKE THE LOG OUT OF YOUR OWN EYE, AND THEN YOU WILL SEE CLEARLY TO TAKE THE SPECK OUT OF YOUR BROTHER'S EYE."
MATTHEW 7:5

I didn't know anything about Mr. Lanfelt except that he was a boozer. He clearly had his own demons to wrestle. Being a grown-up didn't mean you had it all together. I decided to follow Jake's rule and refrain from judging a stranger.

After a while, my brain caved to the fatigue in my body, and I fell asleep.

. . .

I woke abruptly sometime before dawn. After a moment of wondering why I was awake, I heard the muffled sounds of a struggle in the living room. I slipped out of bed to investigate, opening my door and peeking around the corner.

Two shapes materialized in the darkness: Mom and Moses. He had her pinned against the wall, his hand over her mouth and a knife to her throat. Her tears shone in the moonlight slithering through the drapes.

"If you ain't buyin' it from me, you buyin' it from someone else," Moses hissed at Mom. Her gaze darted over to where I stood in the shadows, then back to Moses—almost as if she were scrounging for the last drop of courage inside her, to get him out of the apartment and away from me.

"Not here," she said. "Let's go to your place. We can talk about it there."

"Y'think I'm stupid?" Moses yelled, holding the tip of the knife to her throat until a drop of blood trickled down. "Gonna kill ya both, you and your kid. Thinks she's better than me."

My mind was racing, my heart beating out of my chest. I had to do something. I'd seen Moses cross the threshold from angry to completely crazed before. And that was with guys. There was no telling how far he'd go with a woman who couldn't fight back. Jake had taught me some self-defense moves, but I wasn't sure that would cut it against Moses with a knife. I pushed my fear down; there was no time to weigh pros and cons. I had to act.

I tiptoed to Jake's room and opened the vault. My hands were shaking as I lifted the gun out. It felt heavier than I remembered, but I had no time to contemplate that. All that mattered was that I scare Moses away. I sifted through my memory, finding the moment when Jake taught me how to use the gun.

I left the room and crept up behind Moses, holding the gun in both hands, arms outstretched. I took a deep breath to simmer down the terror brewing inside me. A second's hesitation could mean the difference between life and death. I couldn't let Moses hurt Mom.

"Get away from her," I said. It didn't sound like my voice. The gun gave me power and made me sound more confident than I could have imagined. Moses released Mom and turned, then shrank back when he saw the gun. Mom scrambled away from him and sank to the floor, weeping.

"Calm down. You're gonna wake the neighbors," I whispered. She became very quiet.

Moses tested me, probably thinking I wasn't serious. He even took a step forward like he was going to walk right into the barrel. I'd never wanted to harm a soul, but at that moment, it wouldn't have taken much for me to put a bullet through that horrible man. He was in *my* house, where he had no business except causing harm to Mom and me.

"Look at you, li'l girl!" he said. "Ya even know how that thing works?"

I cocked the hammer like Jake had shown me. It sounded every bit as scary as it did in the movies.

"Oooh, li'l girl real serious now," Moses said, mocking me. But he was less sure of himself.

"Put the knife down," I said firmly. Then I took a step toward him, and he must have decided I wasn't playing. He threw the knife on the floor.

"Easy now, I was jus'—"

I shoved the gun in his face.

"I don't care," I said. "Get out. *Get out!*"

Moses scuttled out the door. Even when Jake was around, Moses had never passed up an opportunity to harass me when I was alone. He pulled this on us now because he thought two women would make easy targets. But while Mom was a mess, every second that ticked by made me stronger and more determined to teach Moses a lesson he'd never forget. My aim didn't waver, even when he glanced back on his way out the door.

I hurried over and bolted the door behind him, then fell against it, shaking. The gun suddenly weighed a ton.

"Are you okay?" I asked Mom.

She struggled up from the floor. "I'm fine," she said.

I was surprised at how clear she suddenly sounded. She put her hand on my cheek, took me in her arms, and held me.

"I'm sorry, baby," she whispered. "I'm so sorry."

I didn't hug her back, not quite ready to release my anger toward her. But we stood there for a while. When my wrists felt too weak to hold the gun, I returned it to the vault. Then I sat on Jake's bed, trying to feel something other than the fire raging within me. I remembered the Native American legend of the two wolves.

One night, about a year ago, Dad had turned everything in my room upside down, looking for a bottle of booze he was sure Mom had hidden from him. He left the broken mess of my inner sanctum behind. I was in a blind rage that day, and it took Jake a while to calm me down. He helped me clean up my room and put things back the way they were.

Still, all I could see in my mind's eye was the chaos in Dad's wake. While Jake and I cleaned up, he told me the story.

"An old Cherokee man told his grandson about a battle that goes on inside all of us," he said. "*My son, the fight is between two wolves. One is evil: he is anger, envy, sorrow, regret, greed, arrogance, self-pity, guilt, resentment, inferiority, lies, false pride, superiority, and ego. The other is good: he is joy, peace, love, hope, serenity, humility, kindness, benevolence, empathy, generosity, truth, compassion, and faith.'*

"'*Which wolf wins?*' the grandson asked.

"His grandfather smiled and said, '*The one you feed.*'"

The vengeful wolf inside me wanted to lash out and find a release for all the fury I'd bottled up over the years. My fingernails bit into my palms as I balled my hands into fists. *Don't feed the bad wolf*, I kept telling myself, until a calm came over me.

I walked back to the living room. Mom was picking up pieces of a broken vase. I didn't know the history, but I knew the vase was precious to her. I got on my knees and helped her.

"Maybe we can glue it together again," I said. "It's all big pieces."

She nodded, and we continued to gather the fragments. There was glue that fixed porcelain. And if you were patient and careful, you could put something back together without the cracks showing too much. A lot like life, I guess.

"Moses was angry because I didn't want to buy pills from him anymore," Mom said as we worked. "I told him I'm done with it, and he didn't like that."

"Okay," I replied. I didn't know what else to say to her. How did I erase fifteen years of emotional neglect by the one person who should have loved me the whole time? My life would have been so much worse without Jake. My heart ached when I thought of the heavy burden he'd taken on to protect me and make my life more tolerable. He gave me the mental tools to work with whatever feelings I had to deal with. Even so, it was hard to balance my emotions right now.

"I called your work," I said, trying to sound calm. "They said you were fired a week ago."

Mom hung her head and started to cry. It came from somewhere so deep that I had no doubt the guilt was eating her up inside. I'd seen her angry plenty of times, but I'd never seen her cry. When she looked at me, I could tell she needed to get something off her chest.

"When Jake died, I didn't want to grieve," she said. "I thought if I grieved, that would make it real. Every day, I woke up expecting it to be a bad dream. When it started hitting me, I took pills. It made life more tolerable, so I took more. I'm not as strong as you, baby. I never was."

I was dumbfounded. *She thinks I'm strong?*

Where had she been the last two months, when I was unraveling and trafficking in heartache day in and day out—until Jake's words came back to me: "Your strength is more powerful than any obstacle in your way"; until I realized that I'd be dishonoring his memory if I just curled up in a corner and gave up on life?

"You have no reason to trust me, I know," Mom said. "I want to change. I wasn't always like this. But I'm done. I'm really done with it all."

I didn't know what she meant by "with it all." Perhaps there was stuff I didn't know about. And I didn't want to.

"Okay," I said. I wouldn't get my hopes up, but I wouldn't throw them away, either. "What do you need me to do?"

"Nothing," she said. "Just don't give up on me."

A drop of blood hit the floor. I noticed a cut on her arm.

"He cut you," I whispered, as if someone might hear.

"Must've happened when I tried to get away," she said. "I'll take care of it later."

"No, wait, it looks deep. Let me clean it and patch it up. You don't want that to get infected."

I rose and found the small first aid kit Jake and I had put together for the house. We bought the old-timey red box with a white plus sign on the lid for two dollars at the Salvation Army store, then Googled the list of things that went into a basic kit. Our red box was now filled to the brim with everything needed to take care of cuts, scrapes, even burns. I sometimes wished for a first aid kit to help heal my heart and mind.

I cleaned Mom's wound, put on antibiotic cream, and used a big bandage to protect the gash. We didn't talk, but it was a comfortable silence. Something in the air had shifted. Mom didn't try to convince me she would make everything right, but she did allow me to take care of her. It was her way of letting me decide how to reconnect with her, in baby steps.

By the time my inner turmoil had settled somewhat, the sun was coming up. I refused Mom's suggestion that I stay home for the day, so she made us coffee and toast. We sat at the table, and she took my hand and said a prayer. Simple and sincere. It felt like a warm blanket folding over me.

"I finished the application for lunch lady," she said. "The decision is in your hands whether you want to give it to them. I won't be angry if you don't want to."

She understood I was reluctant to have her work at the place sacred to my being and my education. I appreciated that she left the ultimate decision with me and decided to see how things played out over the next few days.

CHAPTER 15

I didn't realize how sleep deprived I was until I sat down on the bus. As tired as I was, though, a white cloud of hope hovered in my periphery. I wanted to let it consume me, but fear of disappointment stopped me short.

Before I left the apartment, telling Mom to double-bolt the door and not open it for anyone, I noted the beads of sweat on her face.

"You look sick," I said. "How do you feel?"

"It's okay, baby. I'm just going through some withdrawal; that's all. I haven't been taking the pills for very long, so it's not gonna be heavy. Nothing I can't handle."

I Googled withdrawal symptoms for opioid use and how to deal with them.

"You need to rest," I told her. "And drink lots of water. If you start to feel really sick, you need to call me. Please keep your phone on."

Mom shook her head, again embarrassed.

"They shut down my account. I couldn't pay it last month. I'll sleep some and take care of it later."

At least that solved the mystery of why she hadn't been texting me back.

By the time I left to catch the bus, the adrenaline and caffeine had worn off, and the horror hit me. I'd held a gun to a man's head. If it came down to it, could I have shot him? It scared me to think that I could have. When Jake taught me how to use a gun, he said pointing it at someone should be the last resort. Last night was that, but it seemed the memory would haunt me anyway. I still felt the weight in my hands, the tension traveling from my insides to my fingertips and back again.

But I didn't feel so alone now that I had Malala, Huss, Mils, and Nastasia Strasberg in my club of people who'd overcome considerable challenges to pursue their goals. These individuals' unyielding determination to find something good in the direst situations encouraged me to look deeper within and be thankful for what I had instead of griping about what I didn't have. Like Jake always said, struggling for what you wanted built character and strength.

• • •

At school, Mr. Lanfelt had taken a sudden leave of absence. Everyone else hoped the substitute teacher would be a pushover so we could goof off, but Lanfelt's absence put a crimp in my plans. Here I was, ready to march into his classroom and ask for more information about essay competitions—and he wasn't there. Panic fluttered in my chest. *Is he okay? Why did he leave so suddenly? Did it have anything to do with me saying things I had no business saying to a teacher?*

Monique caught up with me in the hall between classes and hooked her arm through mine like we were best friends. Being friends with one of the school's most popular girls felt good. She chatted nonstop about the upcoming party and her new favorite subject: my makeover. I rolled with it. Her fussing made me feel important, even if it was superficial. Most importantly, it got my mind off the drama at home. There was no one to share that nasty business with because who knew who they might tell? Moses would keep his mouth shut, but anyone I told might tell a teacher, and I didn't want to know where that road led.

"So," Monique announced, "I'm thinking we go kinda classy glam with you. Not trash glam."

"Trash glam?" I asked. "That's a thing?"

Monique laughed at my ignorance. "Don't bash the trash glam, girl. It has its place in the world. I'll tell you who makes trash glam shine: the Kardashians."

"The who?" I asked.

Monique pulled her arm from mine and stared at me in shock. Being Monique, all emotions were exaggerated. "Girl, you are not serious right now. You don't know who the Kardashians are? Get out of here. Don't you watch their show on E?!"

I didn't know how to tell Monique that Dad left with the only TV we had, and when it came to life's necessities, TV shows weren't anywhere near the top of my list.

Fortunately, Monique didn't wait for an answer. She hooked her arm through mine again and babbled on excitedly. "Tell you what. One weekend, we binge-watch it. We can squeeze in at least the first two seasons, and I don't mind rewatching it."

"Sounds . . . exciting," I said.

Monique laughed and shook her head. "You really don't know who the Kardashians are? Wow. That's a first."

Just before I got to history class, I received a text from Mom: "Phone is good now."

My heart swelled. Mom didn't just curl up in a ball and feel sorry for herself; she made good on her promise and got her phone account fixed.

"How are you feeling?" I texted back. Withdrawal was no joke. I worried Mom might get really sick. And right now she was alone with no one there to take care of her.

But she texted back, "Fine, baby. Everything is fine."

"I'll see you tonight. Text me if you start feeling sick."

Doubt bubbled to the surface. I didn't know how long Mom had been taking whatever she'd been taking. *Can she get through withdrawal without giving in to a quick fix?*

For a moment, I envied the seemingly carefree kids around me, though Jake had once told me, "You have no idea what the kids you see every day have to deal with. A lot can hide behind a smile." And I finally saw Jake's point. Until the last two days, I'd thought Tamara and Shiloh were living a dream life. Now I wondered about the other kids I knew. What secrets hid behind their smiles? What were their stories?

Senator Strasberg proved that any challenge could be overcome if you set your mind to it, but I still felt reluctant to share my desire to become a senator. Mom had been adamant that I should be realistic about life and not get caught up in dreams. Then again, that was a while ago. Had she changed her mind? I wasn't sure if I should tell her. The last thing I needed was her inflicting more self-doubt.

· · ·

On my way to social studies, my eye caught a big flier on the hallway bulletin board announcing a statewide high school essay contest. Five finalists would receive a five-thousand-dollar cash prize. If the overall winner had a senior-year GPA of 4.0 or above, they'd get a full-ride scholarship to a local college. Maybe even an avenue to Harvard. I had to read that three times before the magnitude sank in. And it was Mr. Lanfelt who'd told me to watch the bulletin board.

This was everything I needed to go to college and the first time Harvard had entered my mind as a possibility, however slim the chance to get in. My GPA average wouldn't be a problem for most colleges, especially now that I was getting my groove back at school. Even if I lacked confidence in basically everything else, I trusted my ability to score high academically. I didn't have other talents to rely on. Except my writing—which, for this, was the perfect match. But Harvard felt like the moon.

When I was small, I wanted to be a singer because music videos made it look glamorous and cool. Jake didn't tell me outright that my singing was dreadful, but he explained that everyone had a talent, and it was up to us to find out what it was and develop it to the fullest. I insisted that I wanted to be a pop star. So one Saturday morning, Jake took me to a local singing competition. I sang my heart out, but Jake was the only one hollering and clapping when I was done. The judges' faces said it all.

Afterward, Jake took me to the library. It was the first time I'd set foot in one, and I was in awe. He signed me up for a library card and waited while I perused the kids' section. A whole new world opened up to me. On our way home, I couldn't stop paging through the three books I'd borrowed, eager to read them all at once. That was the day I knew I wanted to discover the world and learn everything about it. I put my shaky singing prospects on the back burner. The subtle way Jake quelled my fantasy of being the next Beyoncé still made me smile. He insisted that the world would benefit more from my mind than my singing abilities.

Mom and Dad took it for granted that Jake was a football star and I wouldn't amount to much. The fact that my parents expected nothing from me should have been a relief, but it wasn't. Jake would parade my straight-A report cards around the apartment, but there was hardly any acknowledgment from Mom or Dad. It was like a smart kid with some pipe dream had no place in their reality.

But none of that mattered anymore. I had no one to prove anything to except myself. I knew that I could accomplish anything I wanted to. Even if self-doubt surfaced from time to time.

I took a pic of the essay flier because there was too much information to write down. I'd take a look at the website the first chance I got. This was a once-in-a-lifetime opportunity and would take serious study.

"Are you thinking about entering?"

I swung around, surprised and a little nervous to see Shiloh behind me. After our last conversation, I wasn't sure how our next encounter would go. He'd given me a glimpse of the vulnerable boy under the layers of confidence he always exuded. I tried to gauge his emotional state, but all I could see was the Shiloh everyone knew and loved. He was in charge again, confident and charming. It was like his confession to me never happened. I tried to shake off my confusion.

"Not just thinking about it," I said, doing my best to sound cool. "I'm all in."

"I thought public speaking wasn't your thing," he replied.

That got my attention. Not only did I have a deadly fear of public speaking, but Shiloh remembered me saying that.

"What do you mean, public speaking?" I said. "This is about writing the best essay, not the best speech. Or did I read it wrong?"

"The five finalists have to read part of their essay to an audience," Shiloh confirmed.

"Oh no. How do you know that?"

"I was a finalist last year," he said with a smirk.

A part of me was in awe of Shiloh for reaching the finals. Another part of me was scared. If Shiloh couldn't win this competition, what chance did I have?

"What was your essay about?" I asked.

"Alternative media and independent thought," Shiloh answered. "Boring, I know."

"That's not boring at all," I said. "I'd love to read it."

"One of the judges said it was well written but had no heart. Apparently it didn't hit the right emotional moments. To quote the judge: 'You're a bystander, observing the situation rather than embracing it.' He also thought I approached it with an opinion of my own instead of citing heartfelt particulars about how it affected my fellow humans."

"Then enter again this year and change their minds."

"We'd be competing with each other," Shiloh replied.

"Yeah, you're right," I said, unsure how to deal with the feelings whirling inside me. "Are you entering then?"

"I'm thinking about it."

My bubble of enthusiasm burst. If Shiloh was my competition, I might as well throw in the towel. Why did he even want to enter a competition with a cash prize and a scholarship? His parents were insanely rich. They could afford to send ten kids to Harvard. The rebel in me wanted to confront him about taking the opportunity away from someone who needed it more.

"I'm not doing it for the money or the scholarship," he said, as if reading my mind. "In case you were wondering. I'm doing it for the prestige and opportunity. Winning this competition gets you noticed by people who can help shape your future in whatever career you choose."

"But you still get the money and the scholarship," I said.

"The guy who won three years ago relinquished the prize money and the scholarship," Shiloh said. "So the runner-up got both."

"Good for him," I remarked, then worried the words had come out snarky. Shiloh smiled anyway.

"Hey, I haven't even decided I'm entering."

"As long as you do it for yourself and not your dad," I said. *Was that a low blow?* I worried in a sudden panic. Shiloh got tense; I could see by the way his fingers tapped against his leg and his mouth pursed slightly. We stood before the bulletin board, gazes locked, neither one willing to look away first.

"I'll take that as a challenge," he said. "I mean, how could I not?"

So, even if my comment was intrusive, Shiloh took it in stride. It made me feel exclusive, in a good way. Shiloh had a lot of friends. He was one of the most popular guys at school. But they knew the Shiloh he wanted them to know. It was as if I had a backstage pass, getting a closer look at the boy himself and not just the charming performer everyone else saw on the stage. I didn't want him to regret sharing that side of himself with me.

A few boys gathered to check the bulletin board, likely for sports announcements. A burly guy saw the flier for the essay contest.

"Check this out!" he said. "Can you say Nerd City?"

"Maybe you should enter, Bruno," his friend said. "We'll spot you some crayons and paper." They all laughed, slapping Bruno on the back as they walked away.

A corner of Shiloh's mouth lifted in amusement. "I believe we were just called nerds."

"I'm okay with being called a nerd," I said. "Actually, I'm totally cool with it."

"Well, consider the challenge accepted, nerd."

I flashed what I thought was my prettiest smile. "Sure, nerd. Game on."

CHAPTER 16

I rushed to Miss DeGracia's class with butterflies in my stomach. It wasn't an unpleasant sensation. Most girls strove to be chill around boys, but Shiloh accepting me as his mental equal made me weak in the knees.

Everyone was already seated when I stumbled into class. Miss DeGracia waited patiently while I found a seat. "Let me guess," she said. "Something on the bulletin board held you up."

"Yes!" I replied. I wanted to ask her so many questions, but that should be a private conversation. The last thing I needed was a reputation as a teacher's pet.

Miss DeGracia seemed happier than usual as she asked, "Can anyone tell me the name of the first woman to run for president?" Every hand in the room went up. Miss DeGracia picked one at random. "Cameron?"

Cameron was a big guy with a poor academic record, but he was the junior wrestling state champion and already preparing for the next Olympics. He seemed super excited to answer. "Hillary Clinton!" His deep voice thundered through the room as he turned and high-fived his friends.

Miss DeGracia pulled a comically sad face. "Good guess, Cameron, but not correct. Sorry, dude."

Everyone laughed. Cameron shrugged.

"More than two hundred women have sought the presidency," Miss DeGracia told us. "But not many became their party's nominee. Can anyone tell me who was the first?"

This time no hands went up. I hesitated, not wanting to be that student who knew it all. Miss DeGracia looked to me anyway. "What do you guys think—will Anela once again know the answer? How about it, Anela?"

My cheeks burned, but encouraging looks from around the room gave me confidence.

"Victoria Woodhull, in 1872," I said.

"Thank you," Miss DeGracia said. "That's right. Now, can anyone tell me the name of the first African American nominee for vice president?"

This time everyone looked right at me, and I laughed.

"No pressure, right?" I said. "But okay. Frederick Douglass, who ran as Victoria Woodhull's vice president."

"Correct again," Miss DeGracia said. "Unfortunately for them, women could not vote at the time, and African American men—who could vote—were often prevented from doing so. Which is why most people have never heard of their run for office."

I tuned out for a while. It was all stuff I knew already. My mind kept circling back to Shiloh and the essay competition. There was so much on the line. Winning the essay competition could set up the rest of my life, and everything depended on my topic. It had to be something I could pour my heart and soul into.

I was good at writing as an observer, but opening myself to the world would take substantial nerve. I racked my brain for the right topic. Since it wasn't coming easily, I decided to go to the one place that always served up inspiration: the library where Jake and I had spent so many hours. It was time. I'd go home, make sure Mom was okay, then take the same bus Jake and I always took. There were other libraries, but that one was ours.

The bell rang, and the kids started packing up. Miss DeGracia stood by the door as everyone streamed out. I stopped beside her.

"Can I ask you a question, please?"

"Of course," she said. She waited until the class emptied out and then closed the door. "Is everything okay?"

"Yes, everything is great," I assured her. "It's about the essay competition."

Miss DeGracia smiled. "I'm all ears."

"What do you think are the chances that I could actually win this thing?"

"The chances are excellent," Miss DeGracia replied. "You have what it takes, Anela. You just have to put in the work."

"But what if there were two good candidates from one school?" I asked.

"I think you're worried about going up against a specific student." Miss DeGracia could read me like a book. She once said she saw herself in me, the way she was in high school—always feeling like the odd one out because I didn't go with the flow.

"Shiloh's entering," I said, "and he was a finalist last year. No way I can beat him."

Miss DeGracia bit her lip as if hesitant to let me in on a secret. "Listen, Shiloh is a terrific writer, but so are you."

Even with this ringing endorsement, I was skeptical. My immediate thought was to find some excuse and back out. "Well, I don't know," I said. "The whole 'reading your essay in front of people' thing . . . Public speaking is my nemesis."

A faint smile tugged at the corners of Miss DeGracia's mouth.

"I don't know, Anela. According to Mr. Lanfelt, you had no trouble telling him his alcohol addiction was setting a bad example for the students. So much for being petrified of speaking out."

My jaw hit the ground. "Oh, wow, he told you?" I said, thinking of all the ways I could defend myself. "Did he at least tell you I tried to apologize for running my mouth like that?"

Miss DeGracia looked at me earnestly. "You did the right thing," she said. "You got through to him, and that's not an easy feat."

"What do you mean I got through to him?" I asked. I was baffled.

"He entered rehab this morning for a six-week program," Miss DeGracia said.

"Are you serious right now?"

Miss DeGracia nodded. "Whatever you said to him appears to have worked. And I want to thank you for that."

I stared at her, speechless. *Is she confirming the rumors about her and Mr. Lanfelt being an item?* There was no way to bring that up without sticking my nose in their business.

Miss DeGracia must have sensed my uncertainty.

"We're both very private people," she explained.

I smiled so hard my cheeks hurt. "So, the rumor is true."

"What rumor?"

"About you and Mr. Lanfelt."

I could swear Miss DeGracia blushed. "You're going to be late for your next class."

"Wait, so what topic do I choose for the essay? I have no idea where to start."

"I can't help you choose," Miss DeGracia said. "Nobody can. It will come to you; trust me on that. And, Anela?"

It looked like it was on the tip of her tongue to swear me to secrecy about her and Mr. Lanfelt. I turned as I opened the door to leave.

"Don't worry, Miss DeGracia. Your secret is safe with me."

• • •

By lunchtime, I was exhausted, operating on a few hours' sleep. I didn't like to drink soda, but I needed something with sugar and caffeine. I counted the change in my pocket. One quarter short for a measly soda. My instinct was to text Jake and ask for change. Then reality hit me. Jake wasn't here to bail me out, on anything. I was on my own now.

A feeling of being utterly pathetic came over me, but I quickly discovered another quarter in my coat pocket. I stormed toward the vending machine, fed in my coins, and made my selection. Nothing happened.

It had to look weird, me shaking the vending machine a moment later like I was trying to steal a soda. I wanted to yell that I'd paid and the stupid machine wouldn't cough it up.

Two Bling Clique girls stopped to watch.

"Look," said one, "it's Monique's little rags-to-riches project."

The other one snickered. "Talk about a challenge. That hair alone is a total crime scene."

Anger flared. But I took a breath. If only these girls knew how their privilege protected them. Their biggest problem was what to wear every day. Not where their next meal was coming from or whether some crazed maniac would wake them in the middle of the night and threaten their lives. They'd never know that the girl they were making fun of had held a gun to a man's head a few hours earlier.

The memory of what happened with Moses gave me a rush every time I thought about it, which was often. Sure, I was petrified holding that gun and literally holding someone's life in my hands. But I handled it, and I never backed down. There was too much to lose. So why would I back down when these girls tried to intimidate me? I swung around, uncertain of what I was going to say until the words were on my lips.

"If this is what it takes for you to feel cool, then fine," I said. "But instead of bullying me, why don't you go out and say something nice to someone for a change? I promise, empowering someone will make you feel better than tearing them down."

The first girl sneered. "Freak says what, now?"

Freak? I prayed to keep my presence of mind. There was a life lesson in this moment, but I wasn't sure if it was for me or her. *Should I engage or walk away? Is it even worth trying to get through to her?*

The two girls weren't going anywhere. It was a weird situation. If the soda had fallen into the slot like it was supposed to, I would have walked away. But I wasn't giving up on that soda, so I figured I should be just as determined to persuade these two that no good comes from demeaning others. Maybe it was a lesson for all of us.

"You know what I think," I said, still thumping the machine to make the soda drop. "I think someone in your life makes you feel worthless and small. So it makes you feel good to do the same to others."

The first girl made a pretense of leaving, then turned back. "What would you know about me, freak?"

"Drop the name-calling. My name is Anela."

"Make me."

The soda finally dropped into the slot. I took it out. I could just leave now and stop dealing with the Bling Clique girls. But I stayed and faced them.

"I can't make you do anything," I said. "I can only try to convince you that taking the high road will make you feel better. If someone in your life makes you feel bad about yourself, that's on them, not you. You're so pretty, and I'm sure you're very smart. You have a lot going for you. More than most people. It's in your power to better the world—but only if you want to."

I didn't wait for a reply.

CHAPTER 17

I walked to the cafeteria with my head held high. Opening the soda, I gulped it down. This was the worst way to get energy, but it would have to do.

Hunger gnawed at my insides. I couldn't remember the last time I'd eaten something substantial. The moment I got in line, my stomach growled at the smell of cornbread and chili wafting through the air. The girl in front of me looked around. I expected her to mock me, but she just giggled.

"I'm glad my stomach isn't the only one that's so loud," she said.

"You should hear it when everything else is really quiet," I said. "Sounds like some angry beast emerging from the underworld." We laughed. She moved on to get her food.

I had to stop thinking everyone was out to get me. Jake was of the opinion that the day your attitude changed was the day the world around you changed. If you looked at something negatively and expected it to be bad, nothing positive could wriggle its way through. I felt light on my feet, as if I could feel the world changing around me. Or maybe I was the one changing. Or maybe—like Jake said—it was both.

Gloria, the lunch lady from my neighborhood, gave me an extra helping of cornbread and chili. "You're too skinny," she said. "You need more meat on your bones."

I thanked her, looking forward to the meal.

"Your mom should be proud of herself," she added. "What she did took major guts."

I had no clue what she was talking about. It didn't sound like Mom had done anything bad, but a wave of anxiety swept through me anyway. "What happened?" I asked.

"Oh, girl, this friend of mine texted me that the Italian lady, which could only be your mom, called the cops this morning on that good-for-nothin' manager at your place and told 'em where he stashes the drugs he sells to the neighborhood kids."

I was floored. *Mom did that?* "Are you talking about Moses?" I asked.

Gloria nodded. "Who else? Everyone is so sick of him, but they were all too scared to do anything. But not your mom. Apparently it was a circus when the cops pitched up and arrested him 'cause he wasn't going down without a fight. Now he's in even bigger trouble for resisting and punching a cop."

I must have looked bewildered, because Gloria tapped my hand.

"It's all good, Anela. Nothing to worry about. Your mom did good."

I moved to a quiet corner and called Mom, and she actually answered. I couldn't remember the last time I'd spoken to her by phone, except to leave a message.

"Hey, Gloria told me you called the cops on Moses?"

"I did," Mom said. "I didn't care what he did to me, but I knew he'd be after you next. Not gonna let it happen. He's in jail now, where he belongs."

Warm tears brimmed my eyes. "So, he's gone for good now?"

"He can't even get bail," she said. "It's all good now, baby. We're safe."

"Just like that?"

"Just like that."

"Wow," I said. "Thanks."

"You don't need to thank me, Anela," Mom replied. "You shouldn't have to deal with things like this. That's on me. I'll try to do better."

It felt like an enormous weight had been lifted. And I couldn't get over Mom sounding like she had it all under control. A part of me wanted to stay guarded. Another part wanted to believe things were looking up.

We still had to figure out what to do about rent and bills and keep our heads above water. One solution was for her to work at my school as a lunch lady. If her sudden determination to be a better mom was going to be a thing, she had my full support. I took the lunch lady application out of my backpack and returned to Gloria.

"Um, this is my mom's application for the job here. Do I give it to you?"

Gloria took the application enthusiastically, winked at me, and whispered, "Sure, you can give it to me. I know the kitchen supervisor; she trusts me. I'll put in a good word."

"Thanks. I really appreciate it."

"You're welcome, Anela. You're a good girl. Your mom must be proud. Now go eat your food. It's gonna get cold."

I looked for a seat, amazed at the difference a few days had made. Adjusting my attitude from sullen and feeling sorry for myself to letting other people in. Some kids even smiled at me as I walked past. I smiled back.

Monique waved from the Bling Clique table. "Hey, Anela! Saved you a seat, girl."

The gal from the vending machine was there, looking gloomy. I approached but was hesitant to sit down. Monique grabbed my arm and dragged me closer.

"Someone wants to apologize real quick for being nasty to you." She stared daggers down the table at vending-machine girl. "So, Sandra. What you waiting for?"

Sandra looked up, her face red with embarrassment. Finally, she said, "I'm sorry."

"It's okay," I said. "It's totally fine."

"No, it ain't fine," Monique chirped. "The Bling Clique has a certain moral etiquette. We don't look down on no one, and we build up those with less in life than us. Sometimes a member slips up, forgets that they wouldn't be here without their rich daddy bankrolling their existence. Isn't that right, Sandra?"

I bit my lip to keep from smiling. Monique's honesty was pitiless. She was all about pushing hard love out into the world.

Sandra rolled her eyes. "Whatever," she replied.

"How did you even know?" I whispered to Monique. The last thing I needed was Sandra thinking I ran to Monique.

"Girl, I have eyes and ears everywhere," Monique whispered back. "You handled yourself real good." She looked at Sandra. "To be honest," Monique continued, her tone loud again, "I think Sandra here is jellie 'cause you have Shiloh's full attention."

"What now?" I asked, genuinely puzzled. *How does Shiloh figure in this?* My cheeks grew hot, but I tried to remain nonchalant. "Don't know what you're talking about."

Monique tapped her pink-rhinestone-encrusted iPhone and pushed it under my nose. It showed a pic of Shiloh watching me as I read the essay competition flier on the bulletin board.

"Check out the way Shiloh looks at you, the honey in his eyes," she said. "That's a boy who's sweet on a girl. Veeeerrry sweet."

"Why would you take a picture?" I was mortified. If Shiloh found out my friends were taking pictures of him watching me, I'd never be able to look him in the eye again.

"Relax, girl," Monique assured me. "Actually, I was trying to take shots of the school crest over the bulletin board, to make the Bling wreath for the school fair? We were going through the pics to choose which one, and Sandra here threw a major hissy fit when she saw this."

"Do you have to tell it like that?" Sandra asked. She'd been eavesdropping.

"Girl, you got a better way to tell it? What are you waiting for?"

"Hey," I said, trying to keep the peace. "Shiloh and I were just talking about the essay competition. There's really nothing going on."

"Fine," Sandra said. "Not that I care."

My stomach growled, fed up with not getting the food right under my nose. Sandra rolled her eyes and giggled but shut up real quick when Monique shot her an icy look.

"Eat your food, Anela," Monique said. "Before the wind blows your skinny behind over."

I felt Sandra's eyes on me, so I made an effort to eat like a lady: put a napkin on your lap, wait between bites, hold your fork right, and don't talk with your mouth full. Monique picked up on Sandra staring me down. She hissed to Sandra, just loud enough for me to hear, "You gonna quit being like this? Don't test me. I have no problem kicking someone out of the circle and calling it done."

More of the Bling Clique noisily joined the table. There was a lot of affected chatter, and most of the time I didn't have a clue what they were talking about.

"Moonbeam from Revlon," one of the girls yelled in an argument about the prettiest lipstick shade. Everyone talked over everyone else. Monique smiled at me.

"Not your scene, huh?" she asked.

"Maybe if I knew more about lipstick shades," I said.

"I hear you. There's more power in your nerdy ways than you would ever know."

I wasn't sure what that meant, but I didn't mind being called nerdy.

"So, I have to go somewhere after school tomorrow," I said. "Gonna need your address to get to the party."

"Wait, what now?" Monique asked. "I thought you were coming home with me after school so we can get you all tarted up and looking snazzy."

"How long can it really take?" I asked. "There's only so much you can do."

"Some things take time," Monique said. "Like hair. It takes me hours to get extensions. And I'm not even talking about styling."

I laughed. "I don't need extensions. Please, no."

"You need to be at my house at least an hour before the party starts. I'll ask my hairdresser to stay late."

My mouth fell open. I was surrounded by kids from very privileged backgrounds, but I still couldn't believe how some of them lived.

"You have a hairdresser who comes to your house?" I asked.

"Girl, yes," Monique purred. "Daddy's guilt about leaving us equals lots of cash to fill the empty holes in our hearts."

Even though Monique laughed at her own joke, the truth of that statement was hidden in her eyes. She had everything anyone could ever ask for, but what she really wanted escaped her. It made me wonder: if my circumstances were like Monique's, would I be better off or worse? A little voice told me I knew the answer; but there was also the harsh reality that in different circumstances, Jake wouldn't have had to play football to make Mom and Dad happy. And he'd still be alive. I thought of Marlene, who'd lost her daughter and found comfort in a stranger's smile. What if I'd had a mom like Marlene? But then I wouldn't have had Jake in my life.

"Hellloooo," Monique said, her voice invading my thought bubble. "Girl, where do you go when you switch off like that?"

"I'm sorry. Just have a lot on my mind."

"It's all good," Monique said. "Anyway, I texted you the address. You good for a ride?"

"I'm taking an Uber from Tamara's. Aren't you guys in the same neighborhood?"

"Not walking distance, but close enough."

Someone tapped Monique's arm so she could settle an argument about designer wear. I looked over to where Troy was gabbing with his friends. When I signaled that I wanted to talk to him, he strolled over.

"Look at you, A," he joked. "Hanging with the Bling."

"Funny, Troy. Hey, you remember Tamara?"

"Yeah, I remember her," he said.

"I was just wondering if you'd like to text her sometime."

"C'mon now, A," Troy rebelled. "I know Tamara's your friend, but I got nothing in common with her. What we gonna chat about? Taylor Swift songs? Organic salad?"

I stifled a laugh, but I wanted Troy to get on board with my plan.

"She's sick, T," I said. "She could use someone to talk to, other than me or her mom. She's actually very smart and doesn't like Taylor Swift. She likes Christian rap because it's rap minus the cursing. She loves to read real crime stories and knows every good movie to watch on Netflix."

I made sure Troy understood I was serious; he knew I wouldn't ask if it wasn't important.

"The girl likes Christian rap?" he said. "'Kay, that's kinda cool. I mean, I like it too."

"See, you have at least one thing in common."

Troy laughed. "You're funny. Okay, why don't you give me her digits and we go from there."

Monique jumped into the middle of the conversation. "What are you two cooking up?"

Troy just smiled. He knew to keep certain topics between us.

"Nothing," he said. "Don't you have bigger things to worry about, 'Nique? Like whether your DJ is gonna rock the house or not?"

Monique laughed and playfully punched him in the shoulder. "Why don't you tell Anela what a good time she's gonna have." A moment later, Monique was once again pulled into an argument with her posse, putting Troy and me on ignore.

Troy stared hard at me, looking concerned. "You're going to Monique's party?"

"Yeah, so?" I said defensively. Maybe it was Troy's tone, like he had some say in what I did. I could understand Jake always trying to protect me, but he was my brother. Troy was a good friend who needed to stay in his lane.

"You think that's a good idea?" he asked.

"Yeah, that's why I'm going," I said.

I grabbed my backpack and made ready to leave. But Troy cornered me and shook his head disapprovingly. "Anela, I don't know if you're ready for a party like this," he said. "It's probably not a good thing for you to go."

"I guess that's for me to decide, right?"

Troy threw up his hands in defense. "Okay, okay. Just be careful. All I'm saying."

"I'll be okay," I assured him. "Maybe I'll see you there."

"I'm not going," he said. "I got other things to do."

I felt his eyes on me as I left. For a minute, I considered what Jake would say about me going to the party. He'd tell me I wasn't going to any party on his watch. Troy was probably just doing good by Jake. I turned and smiled at him, waving. Troy waved back, but his heart clearly wasn't in it.

To tell the truth, I hadn't given the party much thought. It felt good to be invited, but I hardly interacted with the kids who were going. I just wanted to fit in. Being Jake's little sis had put me in a safe position at school, but without my brother, it was up to me to prove my worth and carve out a place in the social hierarchy.

CHAPTER 18

My phone dinged on the way to English class. Monique, sending me that photo of Shiloh watching me. I enlarged the image, and my heart skipped a beat. All through English class, I snuck dreamy looks at it. It wasn't fair that I had to have a crush on the one person who could ruin my chances of winning the essay competition. But I put that thought away. It didn't seem to bother Shiloh, so why should it bother me?

When I got home that afternoon, Mom was filling in papers at the kitchen table. She was still pale, and it seemed every minute was a struggle against the cravings. But she had a determined look in her eyes that said there was no more room for failure. I took some Gatorade from the Dollar Store bag and put it on the table.

"Don't know if you like this flavor, but I got you two of these," I said. It was strange to realize that I didn't know Mom well at all. I didn't know what kind of food she liked, what flavor drinks.

"That's great. Thank you, baby," she said.

"They say it's good to keep your energy up. What are you writing there?"

"I'm applying for the management position in the building. Seems there's an opening." The way she said it, with a half smile and a twinkle in her eye, I had to laugh.

"We've been here, what, twelve years now?" she said. "I know this building inside out. It gives us half off the rent. And Gloria called me earlier about interviewing for lunch lady. She said it's as good as done. So, between managing the building, if I get that, and the lunch lady job, I think we're gonna be okay."

I didn't have to sit down and talk to her about how we'd make bills and rent; Mom had thought it through herself. The weight of all that responsibility lifted away, making me feel like I could fly.

"The only thing you have to worry about is doing well at school," she said. "A few neighbors have been dropping off food to say thanks. We're not the only ones who didn't like Moses. I saw a plate of enchiladas, so let's warm some up later and have dinner like a family."

"If it's okay with you, I need to go to the library," I said. "But we can eat before I go or when I get back."

"When you get back is fine, baby."

The bus ride to the library felt strange and empty. I'd never done it without Jake sitting right there next to me. Nothing outside looked familiar, and I realized it was because Jake and I were always talking, so I never really paid attention to anything else. He would try to take my mind off the reason we fled the house, but sometimes questions nagged at me.

On one particularly scary night, Dad had pinned Mom against the wall, yelling at her because she dumped his alcohol down the sink. I was shivering from head to toe afterward, even though it was warm on the bus. I figured it was from shock. Jake tried to calm me down, but getting that image out of my head was hard.

"You can't take their misery on yourself," Jake told me. "It ain't worth it."

"They had to love each other at some point," I said, not sure whether I believed that myself. "Or I don't understand how they got together in the first place."

"There's a difference between loving someone and thinking you love someone," Jake said. He looked at me as if deciding whether he could explain things in a way I'd understand.

"Go ahead. You can explain it to me, oh Wise One," I said.

He laughed and shook his head in mock exasperation, a glimmer of relief in his eyes because I was being sassy instead of acting like a scared little bird.

"Somehow I think you already know," he said. "So maybe you

should tell me."

I had to mull it over. Even if I knew the difference between love and infatuation, explanations were difficult for me. Words flowed easily for Jake, and everything he said made perfect sense. With me, I had to apply some thought to it, and even then I never sounded as wise as my brother.

"I'm waiting," Jake prompted.

"Give me a second," I said. "Okay, infatuation is a physical attraction, and love is knowing someone inside out, the good and the bad, and still loving them for who they are."

Jake seemed impressed. "Wow, that's a pretty good explanation."

"So, what you're saying is Mom and Dad were infatuated and then couldn't sustain a relationship, not to mention a marriage, on that superficial emotion."

Jake raised his eyebrows in awe.

"Who's the wise one now?" he asked. "But yeah, love doesn't judge. Love just is."

I shrugged. I knew the abstract difference between love and in love. But was that enough for me to keep my cool if I fell in love? Less than a month before, I'd bumped into Shiloh and—for the first time—felt butterflies going crazy in my tummy. I'd known Shiloh for over a year, so it was confusing when that feeling of bliss took control of my senses out of the blue.

It had to be infatuation. I knew nothing about Shiloh at the time except that he was Tamara's brother. All I saw was a dreamboat with killer smarts. Not exactly the kind of deep psychological connection true love required.

"But when you're infatuated, it's pretty hard to be rational," I said.

"Are you speaking from experience now, little sis?"

"Promise me you won't laugh?"

"Have I ever laughed when you told me something serious?"

"You know Shiloh, Tamara's brother?" I whispered, as if guarding my secret from eavesdroppers on the bus.

"No way," Jake said.

"Way. I fell hook, line, and sinker. Just like that."

"How long has this been going on?"

"Nothing's been going on," I said. "Except me acting like a fool when he comes within five yards of me."

"Has he shown any interest?" Jake asked.

"No, but it's just a crush. Even if I want to believe it's true love."

"Well, if you ever have trouble distinguishing between the two," Jake said, "ask yourself if you'd still be at that person's side if they became incapacitated. Would you be willing to feed them and change their diaper?"

"Okay, that went dark pretty fast," I said, trying not to laugh. "I'm really not in a place where I want to imagine feeding Shiloh baby food and changing his diaper."

"Yeah, I hear you," Jake said, smiling. "But put it in the back of your mind. Just to keep things real."

. . .

"Hey, young lady," the bus driver called from the front, breaking into my reverie, "isn't this your stop?" That he remembered me from my many journeys with Jake struck me as bittersweet. When I got on the bus this time, he said something about not having seen us for a while, and I had to tell him about Jake. I could see it affected him a bit. He squeezed my arm. The trip felt shorter this time, or maybe it was because I was daydreaming again.

I looked through the dirty window, and sure enough, we were at the library. I thanked the driver and hurried toward the library's inviting light. The chill in the air bit at my nose and cheeks. I was amazed that everything looked the same, even felt the same. That Jake's death hadn't caused some cosmic shift in the world. Just my world.

I tried to ignore the hollowness scraping my insides raw. But the minute I stepped inside the library, a wave of comfort and familiarity flooded me.

The table where Jake and I used to sit was empty. I unloaded what I needed from my backpack and glanced at the counter, where Jake's gaze had always been anchored. And there she was, the girl Jake adored. I wondered if she knew or even cared why she hadn't seen him for so long. She looked preoccupied and not as neatly put together as I remembered.

When she looked up, our gazes met, and she seemed surprised to see me. I tried not to read into it and smiled, then moved on to brainstorming for my essay. The thought of winning the competition made my heart skip a beat. There was an endless list of topics I could write about, and I had to find one that spoke to me. Earlier today, when Shiloh shared the judge's critique of his essay, I had to wonder if that was Shiloh's way of subtly steering me in the right direction. Don't just observe; write from the heart.

I was switching on my laptop when I sensed someone beside me. It was Jake's crush. "Can I sit down?" she asked in a library whisper. "Just for a minute."

"Sure. Of course," I said, a bit weirded out. Questions perched on the tip of my tongue. Did she know about Jake? Was she the mystery girl Jake had been seeing? The one he didn't want to introduce to his crazy family?

She sat at the table, her fingers in a knot. I took the opportunity to get a good look at her. She was mixed race too—a Euro-Asian combination. Her hair was black as night, which made her alabaster skin stand out even more. There was a weariness in her eyes I'd never seen before, but then again, I'd never seen her up close.

"I'm Mayumi," she said. "You're Anela. Jake spoke about his little sister all the time. And of course I saw you here with him."

She spoke of him with such familiarity that it removed all doubt.

"So, it was you," I replied. "Jake's secret girlfriend. He wouldn't even tell me."

"It was because of my parents," Mayumi said. "They were against me dating a guy two years younger who was still in high school. We figured the fewer people who knew, the less trouble we'd have."

It felt strange speaking to the one person in the world who was closer to Jake than I was. I figured they had to be serious, and she hoped to find some comfort by talking to me. But the thing was, Mayumi and I had different memories of the same person, and it was hard to relate to her loss when I still had trouble processing my own. She was a stranger to me, and I didn't know what to say. I didn't want to share my memories of Jake with anyone else. They were mine.

But I suddenly realized how childish that was. Mayumi meant something to Jake, so obviously he meant something to her.

"I know we were young," she said, "but it wasn't just a fleeting romance. It was real. I thought I should tell you. We were going to get married one day."

I was shocked. A life-changing decision that Jake never shared with me. It was beginning to dawn on me that even if Jake was my entire world, his world had been bigger than mine, with more love to share. Maybe that was why he didn't want to tell me about Mayumi. He knew I'd panic about someone stealing him away from me. But now I forced myself to reason the way Jake would: Love wasn't something you rationed out like food. There was no limit to how much love you could give or how many people you could love. Because love was unlimited.

Compassion for Mayumi surged within me.

"When did you find out?" I asked.

"After the funeral," Mayumi said. "I'd been in Japan with my mom for ten days. Jake and I had been texting back and forth, and suddenly there was nothing. No texts, no calls. I knew something was wrong. I found out about the accident online. I just wanted to tell you how sorry I am about your brother. I know how close you two were."

Mayumi was just like me: devastated, her grief still raw. And all this time, she'd had no one to share it with.

"I have to get back to work," she said and stood up. There were tears in her eyes. "It was nice to meet you. Maybe one day we can have coffee or something."

"That would be cool," I said.

When Mayumi left, I felt a strange emptiness, as if we had unfinished business. I tried to imagine how Jake would want me to handle the situation. Should I offer my condolences or friendship to this girl who would have been my sister-in-law, my family? I decided to approach her when she left to go home.

CHAPTER 19

I did my best to clear my mind and work hard for the next two hours while keeping an eye on Mayumi in case she left early. By ten o'clock, the library was silent, and I was the only person left. Another librarian approached me.

"Excuse me," she said, "but we're closing now."

I returned her smile and packed up.

It was cold outside, and I was grateful for the winter jacket and wool cap Tamara's mom had given me. My nose and lips were numb, and I shuffled in place to keep my blood flowing. It felt like forever before Mayumi finally stepped outside. I followed her across the parking lot, feeling like a stalker. I wasn't sure how to tackle the conversation and decided to just do it.

I called her name when she reached her car. She spun around, immediately on edge.

"You'll give me a heart attack," she said.

"I'm sorry. I just wanted to talk some more," I blurted out.

We stood in the cold for a moment. Then she opened her door and slid behind the wheel. "Get in. It's too cold outside," she said.

I didn't need a second invitation and slipped in the passenger side. Mayumi started the car and turned the heater on. As it warmed up, I felt life seeping back into my face.

"I shouldn't have bothered you," Mayumi said. "But when I saw you today, I couldn't help myself."

"It's okay. I understand," I said. "I can't imagine what you had to go through with no one to share your grief with."

Mayumi began to cry. "I don't know what to do with all this pain," she said. "Jake and I had so many plans, even if it meant defying my parents. He didn't want to leave Boston as long as you were here. He even asked me if it would be okay for you to come and stay with us."

Tears streamed down my face. Mayumi took my hand, and for a while neither of us said anything. I felt her pain in the way she clutched my hand. But at the same time, she was trying to comfort me. In her own way, Mayumi's petite size belied her inner strength. We stared out at the nightlife around us, people going about their business.

Mayumi and I both jumped when a homeless man knocked on the window. Mayumi smiled and held up a hand, then retrieved a brown bag from the back seat. She rolled down the window and gave him the bag. He thanked her and disappeared into the shadows.

Mayumi caught my questioning look. "It's just a little care-package thing I have going here. Word has spread. It's just a few things to see someone through another night. Food, water. Sometimes an extra scarf or cap."

"Wow, that's kind of you," I said. "And cool."

"That's actually how Jake and I met."

"I thought you met at the library."

"Well, that's where we saw each other for the first time. But then one night he followed me like you did tonight. When he knocked on the window, I gave him a care package. And he said no, he was here to ask me out on a date because his little sister said he'd be missing the opportunity of a lifetime if he didn't." Mayumi's eyes shone at the memory, and I could see her love for my brother.

"I remember that night," I said. "He told me to hang in the library for five minutes. When he came back, he looked happy. I'm guessing because you said yes."

Mayumi laughed. "You should have seen his face when I held the care package out to him. I mean, it was dark, and I was just used to handing out a package when someone knocked on the window. And there he was, my whole world."

I was beginning to see why Jake loved Mayumi. She was different from the girls at school. Jake and Mayumi shared the same sense of humor and were both kind souls.

"Now that we're talking," Mayumi said, "I have a favor to ask you."

"Sure, anything," I said without hesitation.

"I suppose you have Jake's phone. He took a lot of pictures of us. If it's possible, I'd like to get them."

My stomach dropped. "I never got the phone," I told her. "That night, it was the last thing on my mind, and somewhere in the chaos, it went missing. I asked everywhere."

Mayumi looked horrified. "Someone stole it?"

"I don't know. I never saw it again," I said. The memory of trying to find the phone was painful. Jake's phone would have given me one last bit of him to hold on to, but I couldn't.

"You know what?" Mayumi said. "I might have a way to find it. We had Fitbit apps that were synced up. I'll see if I can track down the last place the phone was when it was still active."

"Wow, thanks. That would be cool," I said.

She put the car in gear. "It's getting late. I'll take you home," she said.

"No, please, you don't have to."

"I want to," she said. "Let me do this. Jake would have wanted me to."

I realized Mayumi was trying to manage her own trauma, and if doing something for Jake's sister eased her pain, I was cool with that. I stared out at all the cars speeding by. We talked about a lot of things. I told her my dad moved out, and my mom seemed set on becoming a better parent. I didn't say anything about holding a gun on a man. I stuck to positive things, like school and the national essay contest.

"Jake always talked about how smart you are," Mayumi said. "How you're going to make your mark on the world. Have you thought about what you want to do one day?"

"I want to become a senator," I said.

"Whoa," Mayumi said. "That's pretty great. Ambitious and cool. When did you decide this?"

"Yesterday," I said, "when we went on a class trip to the State House and watched a live session. I thought maybe I was aiming too high, but then I met Senator Nastasia Strasberg, who really had the deck stacked against her. And I found out many great leaders faced real hardships along the way."

"Well, it seems you've got it all worked out, Anela," Mayumi replied. "Why was the deck stacked against her, though?"

"She's one of the Vietnamese kids rescued from Saigon in 1975. Her parents handed her and her little sister over to American soldiers, begging them to take them to America. She was adopted by a good family in America and went on to become a Harvard professor, then a senator. I saw how she changes people's lives, and that inspired me."

"Were she and her sister adopted together?" Mayumi asked.

"No, that's the really sad part," I said. "She never saw her little sister again. She tried to find her years ago, in the eighties, but no luck. All she has is a picture of them as small kids with their parents."

I saw the wheels turning in Mayumi's head. She seemed glad to be distracted.

"Can you get hold of the photo?" she asked.

"No, but I'm going to the senator's office on Saturday. She has the picture on her desk. I could take a pic of it. Why, though?"

"I'm not a big fan of social media, but it has its uses," Mayumi said. "And if the senator hasn't looked since the eighties, she certainly didn't have the resources we do now. Take a pic and send it to me. I'll put it on Facebook and Twitter. Somewhere, someone might see it and recognize it."

"Should I tell the senator?" I asked.

"I'll leave that to you. But I think no. We don't know if it could lead to more disappointment."

Mayumi pulled up in front of my apartment building without asking for directions. She must have driven Jake home before. She handed me her phone.

"Add yourself to my contacts."

Shock rippled through me when I saw Jake's picture on her phone screen. I'd never seen Jake like that: the way he smiled at the camera, the mysterious glint in his eyes. In that picture, my brother was a man in love.

Mayumi saw me staring. "That was taken the day before I left for Japan," she said. "I wanted his face to be the last thing I saw before I fell asleep and the first thing I saw when I woke up, even if I had to hide the phone from my mom."

I punched my number into her contact list, sent myself a "Hello" text so I'd have her number too, and handed back the phone.

"Call or text me anytime, Anela."

"Same to you, Mayumi. Thanks for the ride."

"You're welcome," she said, then leaned over and hugged me. It was warm and comforting. We shared a last, brief smile before I left the car. Then I ducked my head back in.

"I'm so glad we finally met," I said.

"Same here. It feels like I have a small piece of Jake back."

I felt tears gathering again but quickly wiped them away. "Me too," I finally said.

She watched me until I was safely inside the building. I felt like I'd made a friend for life.

· · ·

In the apartment, I found Mom wrapping the food people had given us in neat little packages to freeze. I didn't know whether to tell her about Mayumi. Lingering doubt held me back. I scanned the kitchen, amazed by all the chow. People had been so scared of Moses for so long—until this petite, Italian woman had made a stand, ready to deal with the consequences if she failed.

But she succeeded, and suddenly Sophia Lee was the queen of our complex. And the way people in our neck of the woods showed appreciation and love was by cooking food. I felt pride at Mom's blossoming and gave her a quick kiss on the cheek.

"So, pick what you want to eat, and I'll warm it up," she said, smiling at my amazement. "We have enough here to last us a couple of weeks at least."

I laid the table, and we sat to eat like a real family, even if it was just the two of us. She asked lots of questions, like I was a stranger and she wanted to get to know me. I told her about the essay competition, Monique's party, and Tamara, all of it tumbling out of me like a waterfall. But I would guard my brother's secret until I was sure Mom could understand why he never introduced her to Mayumi.

"So, this party you're going to," Mom said. "Can I ask where it is, who's gonna be there?"

I laughed at her dipping her toe into motherly concern. It was sweet. Most kids hated their parents stepping into their business, but I welcomed it. *This is what love feels like*, I thought. "It's at Monique's house," I said. "She's dying to glamour me up."

Mom got a little tense at that, but she immediately put her hand on mine.

"Don't know why I'm even worried," she said. "You're such a good girl. I don't think you'd ever do anything stupid."

"I just want to experience it once," I assured her. "Jake hated the school parties, but I want to see for myself. But if you don't want me to go, I won't."

Mom stared at me for a long time. I assumed she was trying to assess how much damage had truly been done to my psyche by growing up in this volatile household. I sat before her, an open book. She could ask me anything, and I would answer honestly. She seemed to grasp that.

"Of course you can go. I trust you completely," she said.

"I have to be back early anyway. I'm working for Senator Strasberg on Saturday. Gotta be on my A game."

Mom shook her head in amazement. "I'm so glad you had Jake on your side, baby," she said, her voice quivering. "Teaching you the things I was supposed to teach you. He did good. Look what a great young lady you've become."

The last thing I wanted was for her to reminisce. Pondering bygones and heartache was what had her popping pills in the first place. She needed to make peace with herself, but that wouldn't happen if she kept opening up old wounds.

"I have so much to learn about you," she said. "Jake had a way of dealing with you, so I stepped back, glad not to have the responsibility."

I took her hand. "It's okay," I said. "We're here now. Think of it as a new start. Let's learn from yesterday and live for today. That's the only way to move forward."

. . .

When I woke up the next morning, the apartment was quiet. I didn't hear Mom moving around and felt the familiar dread that it was all too good to be true. I peeked into her room. She was still asleep, looking peaceful. I realized she was probably just exhausted and needed to rest.

I got on the early bus, where I'd met Marlene the day before. She was sitting toward the middle, an empty seat beside her. "Can I sit here?" I asked.

She smiled and nodded. "You never have to ask."

This time, she promptly spread a napkin over my lap and put an entire sandwich down. It was chicken and mayo. I looked at her questioningly. "Thank you, but we're sharing this. I'm not eating all your food."

Marlene laughed—and took another sandwich out of her bag. "I told my husband about you and how skinny you are, so he made two sandwiches."

We talked about anything and everything. I showed her how to download an app to listen to her favorite church services. We talked about her daughter and about Jake. By the time we reached her stop, it felt like we'd known each other for a lifetime.

School had not officially started for the day, and I always appreciated the first fifteen minutes of quiet before the hallways began buzzing with energy. The early-morning sun crawled up the walls as I passed the school newspaper headquarters. The door was usually closed, but today it was open, and I got my first glimpse of the newsroom. Shiloh read over the shoulder of one of the student journalists as everyone typed furiously on their laptops. The atmosphere hummed.

Ingrid spotted me peering inside their exclusive little world and yelled, "Hey, nothing to see here!"

A second before she shut the door in my face, Shiloh and I made eye contact, and he smiled and winked at me; I was immediately on cloud nine. I had no idea if he considered what we shared romantic or just a kinship of the mind, but there was something special between us. Maybe I could learn to read the signs if I paid a little more attention to conversations around school. Other girls seemed to have a handle on when a guy liked them romantically.

My phone dinged with a text from Mom: "THANKS FOR LETTING ME SLEEP IN."

"YOU NEEDED IT."

"INTERVIEW IS TODAY, WISH ME LUCK."

"LUCK! LET ME KNOW HOW IT GOES."

Having normal text conversations with Mom felt weird. Weird but good. She wasn't pushing me to trust her unconditionally; it was happening at my own pace.

I wandered by the bulletin board with hopes of finding a flier for another essay competition I could enter, one where I didn't have to compete with Shiloh. Of course, there were none. And I only had a vague sense of my topic for the contest, even though the entry deadline was a mere two weeks away—on my sixteenth birthday, no less. That twisted my stomach, but not in a bad way. My entire future was in my hands. It was my responsibility to make this the best possible essay.

Halfway through social studies class, my mind was still on the essay.

"Who can name the three branches of government?" Miss DeGracia asked, strolling up and down the rows. *That is so easy*, I thought. *Why doesn't everyone have their hand in the air?* As usual, Cameron slyly Googled it on his phone. His hand shot up.

Miss DeGracia shook her head. "Anyone can look it up on their phone, Cameron," she said. "I want to hear from someone who doesn't have to Google it."

The class snickered. Cameron pouted, then looked at me. "Not even Anela knows. And she knows everything."

I immediately gauged the temperature to see if Cameron was messing with me. He wasn't. I was in the spotlight. For a moment, I thought to let the comment slide so I could just be "one of the students." But Jake's words came back to haunt me. When I told him I sometimes tried to fit in by pretending not to know the answer in class, he said, "Never stand back, and never concede your worth."

Everyone stared at me expectantly. One girl called out, "Tell 'em, Anela. Let's show the boys the girls are smarter than they are."

A good-natured argument broke out amid a mock betting game, with candy bars and junk food thrown into the pool. Miss DeGracia winked at me.

"Sure," I said. "There's the legislative branch, which makes the laws—like Congress. Then there's the executive branch, where they carry out laws—like the president, vice president, cabinet, and federal agencies. And then there's the judicial branch, which evaluates the laws; that would be our court system."

"Well, what do you know," Miss DeGracia said. "Anela is correct. But before you celebrate, I have one more question."

Another girl shouted, "That's not fair! We already won."

The class was tangled in suspense.

"What do you call the president's power to enact a law?" Miss DeGracia asked.

A palpable hush descended. All eyes were on me.

"It's called an executive order," I said. "No action by Congress is required, and it has much of the same power as a federal law."

The girls gasped and cheered while the boys groaned and handed over their junk food.

CHAPTER 20

I was diligent about getting Tamara's homework assignments to her and taking notes on things discussed in class. I wanted her to return to school without having missed a single lesson.

The lunchtime buzz around the Bling Clique's table was all about who would wear what to Monique's party. I took a seat at the end of the table and ate my food, listening to the happy chatter. My world was a million miles away from theirs, but it was a fun vibe to be part of. Even if all I could think about was going to the State House in the morning and seeing Senator Strasberg again. And I needed to take a picture of the family photo on her desk and send it to Mayumi. I was skeptical about her plan, but Jake would have told me to go for it. To do something good for someone else, even if they didn't know about it.

"Hey, Anela!" Monique called, ripping my thoughts away. "What do you think of this lipstick color?" She pursed her lips at me. I gave her two thumbs-up. She smiled and returned her attention to the other girls. I loved Monique for trying to include me, and I loved her even more for still giving me my space.

After school, I went to the main gate, where all the SUVs picked up the rich kids. My Uber ride awaited me, as promised.

I was relieved to find Tamara's driveway empty. No black Range Rover. The less I had to deal with Tamara's dad, the better.

My plan was to divide the three hours with Tamara into half-hour blocks for different subjects, with occasional ten-minute breaks. I had it perfectly worked out. But when I got to Tamara's room, she wasn't having any of it.

"Anela!" she screamed excitedly. "Guess who texted me!"

I played dumb. "Who?"

"Troy! And we texted for an hour!"

"Wow, that's awesome," I said. I grinned at her happiness.

"You didn't have anything to do with it, right?" she asked, watching me closely.

I chose my words carefully because I didn't want to lie.

"He asked me for your digits," I said. "So, what did you two talk about?"

"Everything! Music and movies, you name it," Tamara gushed.

I kept checking the phone for news about Mom's interview, but there was nothing.

"What are you wearing to the party tonight?" Tamara asked.

"Monique has something she wants me to wear. I haven't seen it yet."

"You know she's going to dress you up in something blingy, right?"

"I don't even know what people wear to these things," I said.

"You can have whatever you want from my closet," Tamara offered. "But I'm bigger than you, and neither of us has the skill to take in a seam. Let's ask my mom."

"Let's not bother your mom. She's done enough."

"Do you want to look good for Shiloh or not?"

"There are going to be tons of people at the party," I said. "Chances are Shiloh won't even know I'm there."

"Shiloh's at a friend's house right now, and they're both going to the party," Tamara said. "Otherwise I would've finagled you a ride with him."

"Look at you using the word 'finagled,'" I teased. "But seriously, you can't push Shiloh to like me."

"I'm not pushing anyone," Tamara said. "I'm facilitating. Like you facilitated Troy texting me."

"You caught on to that," I said, defenseless. "It was done out of love."

"And see how well that worked out," Tamara said with a smile. "Now, let's get this ball rolling." She rang her call bell urgently.

Isabel came running in a moment later. "Are you okay?" she asked.

Tamara squealed, "I'm fine, Mom, but you're gonna have to help us make Anela look smoking hot for a party."

I protested that we hadn't done much in the way of schoolwork, but this was brushed aside.

"Chill, Anela. This is way more important than school," Tamara said.

She and her mom looked me up and down.

"I'm thinking classy, conservative, but not uptight," Isabel said.

"I hear you," Tamara added. "But I'm also thinking smoking hot so Sandra can shut up and stay in her lane."

I'd told Tamara about my little run-in with Sandra, and she was dead set on a little healthy revenge. "As if Shiloh would ever go out with someone as shallow as Sandra," she said.

Isabel was already selecting dresses from Tamara's walk-in closet. Minutes later, she held them up one by one while Tamara picked out the "maybes." When Isabel revealed an emerald-green dress, I fell in love.

"That's the most beautiful dress I've ever seen," I said. It had an old-timey look and was made out of silk, as far as I could tell.

"It would look stunning on you," Isabel said. "Go put it on so I can see if it needs to be taken in anywhere."

I went to the bathroom and put the dress on. Looking in the mirror, I was stunned by the image staring back at me. Suddenly, I wasn't li'l Anela anymore. Even if I was still a skinny thing, I had some curves. I'd never given my clothes a second thought; clean and hole-free was fine by me. But this dress made me feel like a young woman and not just a nerdy girl from the hood. When I showed Tamara and her mom, they both stared at me in wonder.

"You look beautiful!" Tamara said. "That dress was made for you."

Isabel circled me. "Okay, we only need to take it in under the arms and in the middle. I'll let you and Tamara pick out a pair of shoes, but we need to decide what you want to do with your hair."

"We're not done with Tamara's schoolwork," I said. "I don't want her to get behind."

Isabel examined my hair and stood back to take in the whole picture.

"I'd wear my hair loose if I were you," Isabel said. "To frame that beautiful face of yours. Why don't you guys go on with the schoolwork while I do some sewing? Then we'll get Anela ready for the party."

My phone dinged with a text while we were doing algebra. It was Mom: "Guess who's the new lunch lady?"

"That's great! Congrats!" I texted back.

"And guess who's the new building manager?"

"Wow, double congrats! You deserve this."

"Don't forget to send a pic of you dressed up for the party."

"Watch this space," I texted back, including a smiley face. I added a little heart emoji. Somehow I knew that would mean a lot to her.

Tamara touched my arm. "Hey, is everything okay? Why are you crying?"

"These are happy tears," I said. I decided to share everything that had happened over the last few days. The words flowed out of me like water through a burst dam. When I told her about holding Moses at gunpoint, she gasped.

"What if he called your bluff?" she asked.

"I don't know," I admitted. "But he didn't, and now he's in jail."

Tamara hugged me, and I cried without trying to stop the tears from falling.

"No kid should go through the things you've gone through, Anela."

"Jake always said you can use adversity to build character," I replied. "It makes you strong and determined."

"I don't know," Tamara said. "How does that even work?"

"I've wondered how different it might have been to grow up in a place like this," I said. "Never having to worry about food or warmth. But it's just no use pondering life's what-ifs. Jake said it was a waste of time that could be better spent thinking 'how-to' instead. And Senator Strasberg told me about American presidents who used the obstacles in their lives to become strong leaders."

"Okay, but they're boys," Tamara said. "You're a girl."

"I could tell you about a few women who made it pretty far in life despite terrible things happening," I said, happy I'd done my research at the library last night.

Tamara's eyes went wide. "I'm all ears."

"So, there was this girl who was sixteen when she watched her father suffer a massive stroke," I began. "He became paralyzed before her eyes. Also as a teen, she was forced to get married and was then abused by her husband every day."

"Wow, that's terrible," Tamara said. "Who was she?"

"She became the first female president of Liberia. Her name is Ellen Johnson Sirleaf."

Tamara was clearly fascinated, and I was happy to teach. "Then there was Margaret Thatcher, who had to do her schoolwork under the kitchen table because her neighborhood was getting bombed."

"I can't imagine how hard that had to be," Tamara said. "I don't even want to do homework while living my cushy life here."

I laughed at Tamara's honesty. "Okay, then there was the six-year-old girl who watched her father and grandfather get arrested while her mother gave birth to her baby brother. The baby died a few days later. She didn't see her father for much of her childhood because he was in jail. Then she had to nurse her dying mother. Her aunt called her 'ugly and stupid,' and no one stood up for her."

"Who was that?!" Tamara exclaimed.

"Indira Gandhi, India's first female prime minister. There are others, some of them worse."

"Well, you have my attention now," Tamara said. "And this beats doing algebra."

"Okay, another girl was fifteen when a would-be assassin shot at her father, right in front of her. Her father told her not to look as the crowd around them literally tore the man apart, limb from limb."

"Wow, that's gross. How is anyone okay after seeing something like that?"

"That little girl was Benazir Bhutto," I said, "who became the first female prime minister of Pakistan. So when you ask how trauma can build character, those are just a few of the many women who found the strength to carry on and become leaders."

"That's intense," Tamara said. "Does that mean because I'm trauma-free, I'll never get anywhere in life?"

"No, silly," I said. "Not everyone has the same trauma. And didn't you say your illness made you more determined to become a doctor one day? That's a trauma that makes your determination stronger, right?"

"Wow, now that you say it like that. But, hey, enough serious stuff. We should get you ready for the party. I already texted Monique and told her she's off the hook for dressing you up."

Tamara straightened my hair into submission while I texted Monique myself: "I HOPE YOU'RE OKAY THAT I'M GETTING READY AT TAMARA'S."

Monique texted ten hearts back. "YOU DO YOU, GIRL. LOVE YA."

My thoughts drifted to the essay as Tamara and Isabel fussed over my appearance. Excitement filled my whole being. I'd never felt so optimistic about a challenge. Only two weeks remained, but I suddenly knew I could handle it. It all boiled down to me beating the boy I had a crush on.

By the time I was ready to go to the party, I didn't recognize myself. Isabel declared that the only makeup I needed was a bit of mascara and a nice, light shade of lipstick, so that's what we did. Then I had Tamara take a pic of me, and we texted it to Mom. She texted back a row of hearts.

Soon after, Isabel dropped me off at Monique's house—or rather, mansion. My mouth fell open. "I thought your house was huge," I said. "But look at this one."

Isabel laughed. "Keep your phone on and call me anytime."

"Thank you," I said. "I appreciate everything you've done for me."

"You're welcome, Anela. I'm just happy Tamara has you as a best friend."

CHAPTER 21

When Monique opened the massive front door, she stood back to assess my look.

"Who are you, and what have you done with Anela?" she asked. "Yeah, I can see now that the look I had in mind wouldn't have suited you. At all. Girl, you look stunning. Come in. Let me show you around."

Loud music bounced off the walls. The next thing I knew, I was in the throng of partygoers. Monique dragged me from one cluster to another, introducing me to what felt like a million people. "So, this is Anela Lee," she'd say. "Remember the name."

I laughed at the melodramatic intro. "I don't know if you should be telling people that, Monique."

She winked at me. "Girl, you gonna be someone someday. I can feel it. You would too, if you let yourself."

That was deep for Monique. She smiled at my confused expression. "I might be superficial, but I'm not stupid. God blessed you with this amazing brain."

"Thank you," I said. "Your support means a lot to me."

"It's nothing, girl. Just speaking my truth here. Now, get out here and socialize. And don't forget there's some snacks and punch in the dining room."

After a while, the names and faces began to blur, and with everyone yelling over the blaring music, I started to feel overwhelmed. I wanted to be in the library with my laptop, writing my essay.

My mouth was dry, and I thought it was as good a time as any to get some punch. When I got to the bowl, a guy wearing gold chains and low-riding pants moved in alongside me.

"Hello, beautiful," he said, looking me up and down. "I've never seen you at one of Monique's parties before, and I don't miss much. I'm Dwayne."

"I'm Anela," I said. Dwayne was older than most of the teens at the party, and I was a little grossed out. *Why would he greet a girl who is obviously still a kid with "Hello, beautiful"?* This was the kind of guy Jake always warned me about. Dwayne was trying too hard to be charming and engaging. And the smell of his aftershave was overpowering. Another minute, and I'd start sneezing.

"What do you say we go upstairs, away from all this noise?" Dwayne suggested. "You know, so we could chat some."

Out of my element, I played for time, debating how to handle the creep. I took a sip of what I thought was straight punch and, choking on the strong taste of alcohol, unintentionally sprayed red liquid all over Dwayne's white designer T-shirt. The music was too loud for me to hear him, but he was clearly cursing while I apologized. And just like that, he lost interest in me. I threw the punch cup in a bin and searched for an escape to the outside.

I caught sight of Shiloh talking to Sandra by the grand staircase. She was throwing her hair around, pouting her shiny red lips, and laughing at everything Shiloh said. Jealousy heated up inside me. I briefly considered going over there and competing for his attention but then abandoned the idea. Shiloh was still my strongest competition for the most significant opportunity of my life.

I went outside and let the cold breeze flow over me, determined to concentrate on one thing and one thing only: writing the best essay ever. I couldn't let my personal feelings or anything get in the way.

"Anela?"

I swung around to find Shiloh gawking at me.

"Oh, hey, Shiloh," I stammered, completely forgetting the pledge I'd just made to myself.

"Can I just say how beautiful you look?" he said. "I mean, not that you're not beautiful any other time. It's just . . . oh, never mind. You look great."

Shiloh's fumbling made me smile, and my confidence blossomed.

"You don't look too bad yourself," I said.

"Aren't you cold out here?" he asked.

"I was actually trying to escape," I told him. "I wish I was writing my essay in a warm library, if that tells you anything. Nerd alert."

He laughed at my stupid joke, and the butterflies in my tummy fluttered like crazy.

"To be honest, me too," he admitted. "I was guilted into coming to one of these. Now I can say I've been to one, and it's not my scene either."

Sandra traipsed outside, eyes shooting fire at me before she smiled sweetly at Shiloh.

"I thought you were getting me something to drink," she chirped.

"There's booze in the punch," Shiloh said. "I don't think me giving alcohol to a minor is legal."

Sandra exploded, her face contorting with rage. "You two freaks deserve each other!" She stormed back inside the house. Someone peered out the doorway just after, I guess to see what the yelling was about.

Shiloh and I glanced at each other and burst out laughing.

"We were called nerds yesterday," he said, still smiling. "And now we're freaks. So we're either freaky nerds or nerdy freaks. Which do you prefer?"

"I like nerdy freaks myself," I said. It seemed like Shiloh and I were on the same coolness frequency.

"Hey, tell you what," he said. "There's a small bookshop with a coffee bar a quick Uber ride away. You want to ditch this party and go there instead?"

I nodded. He stuck his hand out for me to take, and a thrill zipped through me when we touched. We zigzagged inside, through the crowd, and out the front door to get an Uber. I texted Monique on the way, thanking her for the party and telling her I was leaving.

"Yeah I saw you run away with Shiloh, girl," she texted back. "You two beautiful nerds go have fun!"

• • •

On the way to the bookstore, Shiloh and I joked about some of the characters at the party. I told him about Dwayne and how I'd sprayed red punch all over him. Shiloh thought that was the funniest thing he'd ever heard.

"I'll bet he never had a comeback like that before," he said.

"There should be a warning label that there's alcohol in the punch," I said.

"Agreed, never a good idea to surprise a nerdy freak."

Tucked away in an alley between big buildings, the small bookshop consisted of a few rooms filled with books from top to bottom. There were couches everywhere, a tiny coffee bar, and classical music played in the background. It was perfect.

"It's more of a coffee shop with books to read while sipping your brew," Shiloh said. "But they sell books too. Many are by young, self-published authors trying to break in."

"I didn't know a place like this even existed," I said.

"Don't spread the word," Shiloh cautioned. "Before you know it, the yuppies take over and destroy the magic."

We sat at a small, crooked, corner table. Shiloh ordered two hot chocolates, and we shared a slice of cake.

"Thanks for bringing me here," I said.

"You're the only person I've ever brought," he said. "I honestly don't know anyone else I would want sharing the place with me."

"Why is it so special to you?" I asked, suppressing the giggle that threatened to bubble up.

"It's the only place I can come to write in peace," Shiloh said. "Where I can do what I really want to do."

"And what's that?"

"Write novels," Shiloh replied. "I want to be a writer one day."

I was surprised. "I take it your father wouldn't be happy about that?"

"To put it mildly."

"It's your life, Shiloh."

"Not as long as I'm under his roof," he said.

"Not to sound like an internet meme, but you're in charge of your destiny, aren't you?"

"I know. And I know it sounds naive, but aren't parents supposed to support whatever you choose to do?"

"I wouldn't know," I said, though I was starting to learn what it felt like to have my mother cheering me on. "On the bright side, nothing can stop you from coming here to write. At least until you don't have to hide it anymore."

Shiloh's gaze was intense. "It's like you've suddenly blossomed into this wise, cool girl, Anela. Before, you were always in Jake's shadow, almost like you didn't have an identity of your own. Not that you weren't cool."

"I always had him to fight my battles for me," I said. I was simultaneously pleased and embarrassed by his words. "But I think he taught me enough that I can fight them myself now."

We had a second cup of hot chocolate and talked and talked. Even taking the me-crushing-on-him out of the equation, Shiloh was a pretty marvelous guy. Too soon, it was ten o'clock, and the bookstore was closing. Shiloh offered me his jacket outside and held my hand while we waited for an Uber. The jacket was warm and smelled of him.

"We'll keep this between us, okay?" he said. "Not even Tamara needs to know."

My heart stopped. "Keep what between us, Shiloh?"

"This . . . tonight. Our date."

The butterflies in my tummy fled the scene. I couldn't believe what I was hearing.

"I didn't know it was a date," I said, struggling to keep the anger out of my tone.

"I don't mean to upset you," Shiloh stammered. "But you know how my dad is."

As if on cue, my Uber showed up. I took Shiloh's jacket off and gave it back to him.

"Thanks for the hot chocolate and cake," I managed to say. "G'night, Shiloh." I didn't wait to hear his response, instead jumping into the Uber and shutting the door without looking back.

I went home in a daze. This perfect evening had morphed into a monster clawing at my newfound trust and confidence. *So, this is who Shiloh wants to be? The guy who would forfeit a special bond with someone to appease his bigot father?* My anger slowly transformed into determination. At least it was happening now, before I wasted more time daydreaming about Shiloh—when I should be busy writing that winning essay.

Tamara texted me. "Hey, so Shiloh just texted me asking for your number because he wanted to text you? What's up? He was acting weird."

"Please don't give my number to him," I texted back.

"What happened, Anela?"

"Nothing. It turns out Shiloh and I are not a good match."

"Tell me this isn't going to affect our friendship."

"Of course it won't, silly. Besides, who else is going to teach you?" I added a smiley emoji, relieved that Tamara had my back like I had hers.

When I got home, Mom was still awake and packing new groceries in the kitchen cupboards. She looked at me all dressed up and gave me a hug.

"My beautiful girl," she said.

Her tone had me fighting tears. I wanted to tell her about Shiloh, but the words wouldn't come. I wasn't ready to admit what a fool I felt.

But there was no time to obsess about him. I mentally shifted gears and concentrated on finding the best bus route to Senator Strasberg's office. The online bus schedule was complicated, but I finally worked it out to the last minute. I laid out clean clothes, put my State House entrance badge on top, then went into Jake's room for a decent-looking bag to hold my laptop.

Jake's familiar smell wrapped around me. It was like he was right there, talking to me: "Every day is the first day of the rest of your life, li'l sis. What you do with that is up to you." For the first time, I really understood what that meant. I had the power to make my life better every day.

On a whim, I decided to paint a new quote on the wall above Jake's desk. I'd come across it earlier in the day:

> STILL ROUND THE CORNER THERE MAY WAIT,
> A NEW ROAD OR A SECRET GATE.
> J. R. R. TOLKIEN

Mom came into Jake's room as I was painting and glanced around as if seeing things for the first time. She must have realized it was where her kids hid out when she and Dad got into screaming matches. And if that was the past, then this room and its quote-covered walls represented the future.

I continued painting as Mom perused the quotes. Tears cascaded down her cheeks. I wanted to comfort her but realized that wasn't what she needed. She was grieving over letting her kids down, and for Jake.

"Can I paint something too?" she asked after a while.

I was stunned but quickly recovered.

"Of course," I said, holding out a box with brushes and paint bottles. "What are you going to paint?"

Mom smiled. "Something you said to me yesterday. Can I choose any place?"

"Anywhere you can find an empty spot," I said.

And so Mom painted on the wall next to Jake's bed. She chose bright yellow, and at the end of the quote, she wrote my name in red:

>"Let's learn from yesterday and live for today.
>It's the only way to move forward."
>Anela Lee

I went to bed thinking about the "date" and fighting the turmoil inside me. I wished I knew how to stop the sharp pain in my chest every time I thought of Shiloh.

CHAPTER 22

I woke to the smell of freshly brewed coffee and shut off the alarm. Usually my mind would be busy with the clutter of nightmares, but the only dream I remembered was of me being at school, waving to Jake in the distance. That could only mean that I was making peace with Jake's absence. Even so, I felt his spirit was with me—and always would be.

I showered, dressed, and once again confronted the dilemma called my hair. Mom knocked on the door.

"You can come in," I said.

"I'm gonna make you some scrambled eggs," she said. "You're going to the State House with a full tummy."

"Thanks!" I said. "Just give me a minute so I can put some order in this mess."

Mom lingered behind me and touched my mop. "If you want, I can comb your hair for you," she said.

"Sure, but I warn you now: this hair is a challenge." It was strange having to warn my own mom about my difficult hair. But she combed it with confidence and ease. Minutes later, she'd made a bushy ponytail and gelled the rest down neatly.

"Wow," I said. "How did you do that?"

"I watched a few YouTube videos. Happens I'm not the only parent who has a child with wild and wonderful hair."

• • •

When I got to the State House, my spanking-new badge got me right through security. Senator Strasberg's office wasn't easy to find without a guide, but after several wrong turns, I finally found myself at her door. I knocked.

"Hello, Anela dear!" she greeted me.

"Good morning, Senator Strasberg," I said, relieved that she looked happy to see me.

"Please call me Nastasia; formality has no place among friends."

She showed me how she wanted her books arranged. I would also catalog several boxes of new books on the floor. I couldn't see the whole thing taking more than a few hours and tried to hide my disappointment. This was a one-day job.

It was like Nastasia read my mind.

"If you're willing to come every week," she said, "that would be wonderful. By Friday, all those books will be back on the floor, and new ones will come in."

I grinned. "Willing? I'd be totally happy to."

Nastasia completed a brief while I organized the books. We worked in silence, and I loved it. I usually had to listen to loud music to distract myself from the noise outside the apartment, so this was bliss. It also gave me space to think, and despite my best efforts, thoughts of Shiloh and how our date ended crept into my head.

I replayed the scenario over and over. Was I overreacting, or was Shiloh not the guy I thought he was? From what I knew of his father, he wasn't a man to trifle with. But was he the only reason Shiloh didn't want anyone to know about our date? After examining things from every angle, I decided to waste no more time pondering the hows and whys.

At noon, Nastasia ordered sandwiches and invited me to sit at her desk.

"So, Anela," she said. "Tell me about something good that happened to you this past week."

I didn't know where to start. There was no way to explain that my entire life had changed in a week, all because I heard Jake's voice again. And because I realized that I couldn't wait for others to change;

change started with me. So I kept my answer simple.

"I'm entering an essay competition that could change my life," I said. "If I win and keep my GPA at 4.0 or better, I'll get a full scholarship to a local college and maybe a shot at Harvard."

"That sounds terrific," Nastasia said. "Do you know what topic you want to write about?"

"I'm thinking about it all the time. Miss DeGracia said it would come to me."

"Any topic you choose should be personal," Nastasia said. "Even if you choose to write about melting ice caps. It's one thing to sit in a cozy room in Boston, describing the climate horrors befalling the world as the ice caps melt. What matters is making it hit home with the reader.

"What kind of world are we leaving behind for future generations? For our children and their children? Make it personal for the reader as well. Then suggest a solution. It doesn't have to be big. Minimizing one person's carbon footprint can persuade others to do the same. And before you know it, we're all working together to keep the planet livable for future generations."

"Wow," I said. "That was amazing, the way you just came up with that."

Nastasia smiled. "One thing you learn as a senator is to think on your feet."

I told her I'd researched some of the female leaders on her wall and how their roads to success were spiked with obstacles. I admitted I still couldn't relate to their situations but was beginning to see that whatever the trauma, it could be used as a stepping stone to better things.

"What kind of trauma can you relate to, Anela?" Nastasia challenged me.

"I don't know," I said. "Some of these people went through a lot, and I don't think I should compare my life to theirs."

"Everyone has trauma they can relate to," she said. "And minimizing your own holds you back, don't you think?"

It wasn't Senator Strasberg I was talking to anymore; it was Dr. Strasberg, the psychologist. I wondered what Miss DeGracia had told her about me. Of course I'd had trauma in my life, but I didn't think the world was interested in knowing about it.

"You're right," I admitted. "My brother told me that suffering should be seen as a stepping stone and not an excuse or a hole that pulls you down into darkness."

"Your brother sounds very wise," Nastasia said.

"He died a little over two months ago," I blurted out. "He was my rock because my parents were . . . not there for me."

Nastasia abandoned her sandwich and rose to stand by the pictures of twelve boys. She pointed to a chunky but self-assured-looking teenager in a Western fringe shirt.

"Any guess who this is?" she asked.

"I assume he was a president at some point," I said with a smirk.

Nastasia smiled at my wisecrack. "Let's call him by his birth name, Blythe. At three, he was living with his grandparents because his mother went to school in another state, learning to be a nurse anesthetist."

"Where was his dad?" I asked.

"He died three months before Blythe was born. His car went into a ditch full of water, and he drowned. Blythe later said, 'His memory infused me, at a younger age than most, with a sense of my own mortality. The knowledge that I, too, could die young drove me to try to drain the most out of every moment of life and to get on with the next big challenge. Even when I wasn't sure where I was going, I was always in a hurry.'"

Here was another moment to ponder the power of perception. I hadn't been able to put it into words, but since hearing Jake's voice again, I'd felt the same way Blythe had. Life moved fast, and I owed it to myself—and my brother—to live my life to the fullest.

"His father's death left Blythe with no consistent father figure," Nastasia continued. "He was bullied, even by his first stepfather, Roger."

"Did his mom step in and protect him?" I asked.

"Well, his mother was bullied too, and was afraid of Roger. When Blythe was five, his mother wanted to see her grandmother in the hospital. Roger told her she couldn't go, and the two of them got into a screaming fight. When Blythe approached the doorway, a gun went off. The bullet hit the wall right next to him. Roger was trying to shoot Blythe's mom. She grabbed Blythe and ran across the street to a neighbor's house."

I assumed Blythe was someone who went on to do great things, so it was strange to see a resemblance to my own upbringing in the story of his childhood. I couldn't wait to find out who he was.

"What happened to the stepfather?" I asked.

"He spent a night in jail."

"That's it?" I said. "One night?"

"One night. As you might expect, that didn't stop things. When Blythe was fourteen, he found Roger standing over his mother, beating her, so he grabbed a golf club and told Roger he'd beat the hell out of him if he didn't stop right then."

"What happened?"

"Roger stopped. The police again took him away for the night. Another time, Roger bent Blythe's mother over a washing machine and held a pair of scissors to her throat. Blythe pulled her away and, while standing between them, told Roger he'd have to kill him first. He was sixteen then and already bigger than his stepfather, so Roger backed off."

"I didn't go through what Blythe did," I said, "but I feel I can relate in some way."

"Later in life, Blythe acknowledged that everyone has a story—of dreams and nightmares, hope and heartache, love and loss, courage and fear, sacrifice and selfishness. He wanted to grow up to serve and give 'people a chance to have better stories.'"

"Now I'm really curious," I said. "Who did Blythe grow up to be?"

"William Jefferson Clinton. Or President Bill Clinton, as most know him."

"Where did the name Blythe come from?" I asked.

"William Jefferson Blythe III was his name at birth," Nastasia said.

That got me thinking. *If all of these people were traumatized as kids, how many others didn't become famous? How many had a hard time getting ahead in the world?* My heart skipped a beat.

"Blythe's story resonates with me," I said.

Nastasia held my gaze. "So, are you still wondering what topic to use for your essay?"

It took me a minute to realize what she was saying.

"It's staring me right in the face, isn't it?" I said.

"I'd say so, Anela."

Sometime that afternoon, Nastasia said she needed to go to the State House's main library. She gave me her phone number and told me to text her if anything came up. I was amazed she was letting a stranger stay in her office. Even more astonishing was that I had a senator's private phone number in my contacts. That brought a smile to my face.

While she was gone, I took a picture of the framed photo on her desk, of her Vietnamese family. It was surprisingly tricky to get a clear shot with no reflections. When I finally did, I sent it to Mayumi.

"Got it, thanks," she texted back. "Have news on where J's phone is."

My heart skipped a beat. "Seriously?" I texted.

"Seems it was misplaced by paramedics in the chaos to get Jake to the hospital."

"I'll get my mom to pick it up, and then we can get together so you can save what you want from it," I responded. I guess it shouldn't have felt strange that I was so at ease with Mayumi. *Of course* Jake's chosen girl would be someone I liked.

When Nastasia returned, I announced I was done with the books.

"I have a quick question if you don't mind," I said.

"Of course. I'm all ears."

"I have this fear of public speaking. And if I get to the finals, I'll have to read part of my essay to an audience. Do you have any advice about that?"

"Practice. That's all it takes. Ask Miss DeGracia if you can talk about something in front of the class. It's important to engage with your audience. Make eye contact. And know your subject."

"You made it look so easy the other day in session," I said.

"Years of practice," Nastasia replied. "The first time I had to lecture in front of a class at Harvard, I was trembling. Until I realized they were there to learn from me, so I had nothing to be afraid of."

• • •

I worked on my essay on the bus back home. As proficient as I was at writing essays, this one was different. I had five thousand words to splay my heart across the page and engage the reader from beginning to end. Using trauma to better one's life was a tough subject. I hoped to make other kids in traumatic situations aware that they weren't alone; they had options.

Jake's voice gently steered me in the right direction as I made notes.

CHAPTER 23

When I got home, Mom was working on an old computer at the kitchen table. She looked happy to see me. What a difference it made coming home to love.

I raised an eyebrow at the computer, which took up half the table.

"Management company gave this to me," Mom said. "Makes it easier to keep up with rent payments and other accounting."

"We should look for a used laptop somewhere," I told her. "That thing is from the Stone Age. It takes up half the room."

Mom laughed. "It's okay for now. I'm doing an online accounting course. Didn't think I'd like it so much, but I do. How was it working for a senator?"

"I loved it! She's a great person," I said. "You should totally meet her."

Mom's eyes lit up when I said that. "That sounds good, baby. How about some dinner? Then we can relax and watch a movie."

"We don't have a television," I said, thinking she'd forgotten that Dad took the TV with him when he left.

"Look in the living room," she said with a smile.

I peeked around the corner and spotted a modest plasma set up in front of the couch. It wasn't new, nothing grand, but it was fine for watching movies.

"Picked it up at the Salvation Army for next to nothing," Mom said. "Now we can watch movies and eat popcorn on Saturday nights."

. . .

For the next two weeks, I worked on the essay every chance I got, including lunchtime. Monique coached the Bling Clique table into bringing me things to eat and drink. Research took more time than anything else. Eventually, I noticed that Sandra was missing from the clique. When I asked Monique, she shrugged and rolled her eyes.

"Girl has no desire to change her ways. She's all about being nasty. It's not the Bling Clique's way. Don't be worrying about her now. All you gotta do is win this thing."

I went out of my way to avoid Shiloh. Once I made it clear to Tamara that he and I would never be an item, she stopped pushing. I was persistent with her lessons, and her health was getting better.

My heart still beat in my throat every time the Uber dropped me off at her house. I might have decided that Shiloh didn't deserve my love, but that didn't mean I cared for him any less. I didn't know whether to be relieved that I never ran into him. I hadn't told anyone about my "date" with Shiloh, the secret little bookshop, or that some nights I cried into my pillow.

At least I had the essay to concentrate on. It took over my life. Mom made me dinner and tea at night and dragged me to bed around midnight.

"Your brain needs rest," she would say. "Gotta take care of yourself."

I didn't see Mom much at school since she worked in the kitchen and only came out to replace containers. But when we did see each other, I smiled and waved. The kids loved that my mom was in charge of the cafeteria menu, and I got daily requests to pass along.

"Okay, you need to tell Sophia that her mac and cheese rules," one kid said.

"Clearly you haven't tasted her spaghetti and meatballs," another argued.

When I told Mom about that, she was tickled. Jake would have been so happy and proud of us.

On my second Saturday working for the senator, I showed my ID at the State House, and the guards greeted me like I'd been going there for ten years. Of course, Senator Strasberg was already hard at work. She pushed a mug of coffee my way, handed me a donut, and told me to forget about the books and work on my essay.

"If you need to ask me anything, I'm right here," she said.

"Maybe you could tell me more about those boys on your wall," I replied.

She responded with a wide smile. "I thought you'd never ask. Pick one and let's go."

I chose a black-and-white picture of a boy who looked about sixteen. He was in football gear, with a helmet tucked under his arm.

"Ah, good choice," Nastasia said. "You might relate to him more than you think."

On my last two visits, she'd quizzed me about my home life, so I was curious to see what she thought a president and I might have in common.

"Mils, whom you know as President Nixon, had a friend called Dutch. When Dutch was young, it was his dream to become a sports broadcaster. His father was a shoe salesman who had a hard time staying in one place and keeping a job, so the family moved from town to town. In fact, between the ages of six and ten, Dutch moved to a different school every year.

"Life was unpredictable for Dutch, but his mother, Nelle, gave him stability. She was a devoted Christian and taught him how to pray. Dutch said she encouraged him 'to have dreams and believe he could make them come true.' But there was a dark side to Dutch's family. His father was a drunk.

"One cold winter's night when Dutch was eleven, he came home from an event at the YMCA. As he walked up the front steps, he tripped over what he called 'a lump near the front door.' He looked down and found his father, Jack, passed out, 'lying in the snow, his arms outstretched, flat on his back.' He was snoring. Dutch leaned over and smelled whiskey."

"I can imagine how helpless Dutch felt," I said. "No kid ever gets used to seeing a parent like that."

"Well, Dutch thought about ignoring him and going to bed," Nastasia said. "But he didn't. He reached down, grabbed his father's coat, and helped him into the house. Dutch didn't understand why his father had such a hard time with alcohol or why he let addiction control his life and negatively impact the family. But Nelle taught him 'that God has a plan for everyone and that seemingly random twists of fate' happened for a purpose.

"Despite all the setbacks, Dutch still had his hopes pinned on a better life. He was a college graduate during the Great Depression and kept being turned down for jobs. But he kept looking and eventually found a job at a radio station. Dutch became a sports broadcaster, realizing his dream. He became a movie star, too. And, eventually, he became President Ronald Reagan."

• • •

On the morning of my sixteenth birthday, the essay sat in a big envelope on the kitchen counter, stamped and ready to go. Mom woke me with hot chocolate.

"Happy birthday, my sweet baby," she said and handed me a small gift. It was wrapped with care and even had a bow with tinsel. Inside the tiny box was a thin gold necklace with a locket. When I opened the locket, I found a picture of Jake, exactly how I remembered him: big smile, eyes holding a thousand secrets. I shifted into Mom's arms, and she let me cry.

On the days Mom worked as a lunch lady, we rode the city bus together. Today I introduced her to Marlene, and it turned out they'd grown up in the same area. Soon they were laughing and sharing stories of the neighborhood back in the '90s, leaving me alone with my thoughts.

Is Shiloh's essay also in an envelope, ready to be mailed? I was curious about his chosen topic and how he felt now that it was done. Mom would mail my essay on her break. The five finalists would be announced in a month. I had a ton of things to keep me busy 'til then, but I knew it would be the longest month of my life.

At lunch, the Bling Clique surprised me with a small party. Mom baked a beautiful cake and brought it to the table with sixteen burning candles. Even Troy and his football buddies joined in. After a while, he pulled me aside and handed me a thick envelope.

"Here's something me and the guys got together for you. You helped a lot of them with essays and stuff."

"Troy, I appreciate that, I do, but I'm good with money. Mom's working two jobs, I'm teaching Tamara—"

"Don't wanna hear it, A," Troy said. "Not like you'd tell me if you did need it. And you're gonna do fine with the contest. I can feel it."

I accepted the envelope. "Thanks, Troy. I appreciate it. And by the way, you were right about the party the other week. Not my thing."

"But at least now you know," Troy said.

Monique called me back to the table. "Girl, lunchtime's almost over, and you got a ton of prezzies to open. Come."

My birthdays used to be on the down-low, though Jake would fuss and make them special anyway. I didn't know what to do with the sudden attention. I caught Mom looking at me from the other end of the table as she cut the cake. Maybe she sensed how strange this scenario was to me. She winked and blew me a kiss—and my anxiety melted away.

Afterward, I found a small white rosebud sticking out of the vent on my locker door. There was no note, just this perfect little bud about to open. I carefully took it out, placed the bud stem inside the water bottle from my backpack, then put it in my locker to take home later. I wondered if it was from Shiloh.

Hard as I tried not to let it, my mind circled back to that rosebud for the rest of the day. No one except Tamara knew I loved little white rosebuds. Even after I'd told her it would never work between Shiloh and me, she was still trying to manipulate a courtship between us.

I couldn't get mad at her; I knew she meant well. But until Shiloh stood up to his father, the effort was moot.

• • •

One morning nearly a month later, my phone dinged with a text from Mayumi: "Might've found the senator's sister!"

I'd almost given up hope after all this time with no bites. My fingers couldn't type fast enough. "What? Are u kidding me!?"

"Following up with a message on Facebook!" Mayumi texted back. "Will let you know as I get more info."

She called me an hour later. She had found Nastasia's Vietnamese sister, Hien. Hien worked as a doctor at a small-town hospital in Nebraska, of all places. A nurse working with Hien saw the image on Facebook and thought it looked like the photo Hien kept inside her locker door at the hospital. When the nurse asked about the picture, Hien said it had been found in her coat pocket when she came to America from Saigon as a little girl. Her adoptive parents preserved it for her and kept her name, the only thing written on the back.

"Do you think the nurse could get us a pic of Hien?" I asked Mayumi. "And a phone number? We should put them in touch."

Two days later, Mayumi texted me a photo of Hien. It was like staring at Nastasia Strasberg's mirror image.

"Okay, these two are sisters," I texted Mayumi.

"I had the same thought," Mayumi texted back. "I mean, they look like twins."

"This is great. Thank you for doing all this."

"You're welcome. We're family. That's what family does."

Those words made my heart soar. Even though Jake was gone, his influence remained. And he'd loved the perfect girl, who now viewed me as a sister.

Saturday couldn't come soon enough after I decided the information about Hien needed to be shared with Nastasia in person.

That morning, I'd barely knocked on her office door when she called out, "Anela, is that you, dear?"

I rushed inside, catching my breath. "Hi, so, I have something to tell you."

She pushed a Starbucks cup my way. "We're going fancy this morning. I hope you like caramel in your coffee."

"Thanks," I said. "I got us some fresh donuts."

I took two brown bags from my backpack and gave one to her.

"So, what is it you want to tell me?" she asked.

I took a sip from my caramel coffee. "We . . . my friend and I, we think we found your sister," I said carefully.

Nastasia paled. "Is this a joke?"

"No, it's not," I said. I opened Hien's picture on my phone and showed it to her. She took the phone and stared at it as if seeing a ghost, absorbing every little detail.

"She's a doctor at a hospital in Nebraska," I said. "I have her number for you. We haven't said anything to her yet. I wanted to come to you first."

"How did you find her?" Nastasia asked. The usually calm senator seemed flustered.

"I took a picture of the photo on your desk, and my friend Mayumi put it on Facebook about a month ago. A nurse who works with Hien recognized it from a picture in her locker. It was found in Hien's pocket."

Nastasia couldn't look away from Hien's photo. "I can't help but wonder if she looked for me, too. She was a baby. I was a year older, and I can hardly remember."

"If she keeps the photo in her locker, it must mean something to her," I said. "I think she'd love to find her sister."

Nastasia regarded me with tears in her eyes. "You're probably right. I'll call her today. And, Anela? Thank you. You have a kind heart. You'll make your constituents a great senator one day."

The bus was fairly empty on the way home. I was playing Scrabble on my phone when Mom texted me: "It's here."

My heart went into overdrive. I didn't have to ask what she was talking about.

"Have you opened it?????" I texted back.

"Thought I should wait for you."

"Okay."

Tamara texted me five minutes later. "Have you gotten your letter yet?"

"No, but my mom says it's at home," I texted.

There was a long silence; then she texted again. "Shiloh is a finalist."

Those four words crushed any hope I had. No way could there be two finalists from the same school in the entirety of Massachusetts. I was in a daze, my fingers on autopilot as I texted her back.

"Tell him I say congrats."

"Tell your mom to open the letter," Tamara insisted.

Tears burned my eyes, and my insides tied in that familiar knot of stress.

"No way are there two finalists from the same school," I texted back.

"Open. The. Letter."

I texted my mom to open the letter.

It took all of twenty seconds before she texted back, "CONGRATS BABY, YOU ARE A FINALIST!!!!!"

The bus pulled up to my stop. Mom was waiting in front of the building with the letter in her hands. I ran into her arms, and we both bawled our eyes out.

When I finally read the letter, I realized why Tamara had insisted I open it. The other four finalists were listed at the bottom. Tamara had known I was a finalist but wanted me and Mom to find out on our own. I'd never appreciated Tamara more than at that moment.

"You're all kinds of awesome, you know that," I texted.

Tamara texted right back. "I know you don't want to hear this, but Shiloh actually told me you were a finalist before he told me he was one too."

My heart fluttered. *Why does Shiloh's reaction hit me so hard?* I'd done everything in my power to banish him from my thoughts—unsuccessfully.

By Sunday afternoon, the entire neighborhood knew, courtesy of a proud mom. I couldn't poke my head out the door without someone yelling: "Go, Anela!"

The principal made an early-morning announcement on Monday about Shiloh and me becoming finalists. By lunchtime, everyone knew who Anela Lee was. Standing in the lunch line, I had students walking by and high-fiving me or inviting me to sit with their groups. As always, Gloria doubled my portions. She beamed at me.

"You did good, girl," she said. "You did very good."

"Thank you," I said. "That means a lot to me. You know, it's my mom's birthday in two weeks. I want to give her a surprise party. Will you help me with that, please?"

Gloria patted my arm. "Don't you worry about anything. I'll get everybody to bring something to eat, and I'll bake a cake. We can have it in the little courtyard. My husband will string up some Christmas lights, and my daughter can bring her boom box."

I laughed. "Gloria, you should be running your own party business. You're really good at this."

"You think so? I wouldn't know where to start with that."

"You start by making fliers to put up in the neighborhood, offering to do parties."

"Listen to you. But sure, that's a deal," Gloria said. "Now go put some meat on those bones. Don't want the judges to think we're not feeding you."

I joined the Bling Clique at their usual table. It was a buzzing beehive of what I should wear to the event in Cambridge, where the winner would be announced. Monique showed them a pic of me at the party. The emerald silk dress won, hands down.

After lunch, Monique pulled me aside. "I know with your pride and all you're gonna give me lip, but here's some spending money for the trip to Cambridge. For you and your mom. Okay?" She texted me the info.

I wasn't going to argue with Monique. Instead I said, "Thanks, Monique. I really appreciate this. One day, I'll do something for you."

"Girl, you got me reading books now," she said. "Bling Clique is about to start their own book club. It ain't Shakespeare, but you got us reading. You brought some nerd glam to the group. So I'd say you've done more than your fair share."

In social studies, Miss DeGracia didn't make a big thing out of the essay because she knew I'd be embarrassed by all the attention. Instead, she insisted on making me a confident public speaker. I had to overcome my fear of public speaking before the trip to Cambridge. She picked up right where Senator Strasberg left off with the twelve boys.

"Who can give me an example of a president who didn't have it easy as a kid?" she asked.

No hands went up. I knew where this was going. I bit my lip, wishing to shrink to molecule size.

"Anela?" Miss DeGracia said finally. I looked up. "Why don't you stand in front of the class so everybody can hear you."

I thought fast and shuffled to the front of the class, my insides churning. I remembered what Nastasia told me: *Engage with your audience, make eye contact, know your subject.*

I stood straight and looked my fellow students in the eye, but all that came out was "Um . . ." The class laughed good-naturedly.

Miss DeGracia stood at the back of the class, reassuring me with a smile. I remembered something else Nastasia had told me: the students were there to learn from me, and I had nothing to fear.

"There once was a boy," I said. "Let's call him Fitz. Early on, he had abandonment issues related to his mother, Beth. Fitz wanted to be a writer. As a boy, he lived in Massachusetts, New York, and Connecticut. His mother took long vacations while Fitz's dad, Patrick, was away on business, so Fitz and his siblings were often left with people hired to care for them. One day, when Beth announced she would be away for six weeks, little Fitz said, 'Gee, you're a great mother to go away and leave your children all alone!'"

The students laughed at my reenactment. Their expressions urged me to continue, and my confidence grew as I spoke. "Fitz was the second child," I said. "He had eight siblings. Their mom rarely saw them, never kissed them, and shied away from touching them. Fitz told a friend that despite his sadness at never seeing her while at boarding school, he learned to 'take it in stride' because 'his tears irritated her and made her love him less.'"

"Wow," one of the boys in class said. "That's the last time I complain when my mom wants to kiss me goodbye at drop-off."

"Fitz suffered a lot of illnesses, starting at age two," I continued. "He also had a slight deformity. His left leg was half an inch shorter than the right, giving him an uneven gait and twisting his spine slightly, making it unstable. His whole life, he had to wear a corset brace to support his lower back and a quarter-inch lift in his left shoe heel to make up for the short leg. He was always aware of his mortality, even as a child. And that's not a tenth of the stuff that happened to him and his family. But it only increased his desire to live with courage and daring.

"Can anyone guess who Fitz was?" I asked.

The students seemed really curious to find out who I was talking about. I heard a few whispered discussions. Miss DeGracia smiled and gave me a thumbs-up.

"Oh, come on. Tell us!" one kid yelled.

"Okay, okay," I said, laughing. "President John Fitzgerald Kennedy. JFK."

CHAPTER 24

I divided Tamara's latest lessons into time slots, but the minute I arrived at the house, I knew there would be no lessons. Isabel sent me a link to videos of all the previous finalists reciting their essays to the audience and said Shiloh was on last. The butterflies awakened in my stomach. "You can watch them later," she said.

Oh great, I thought, *now I have a video of Shiloh reciting an essay*. Of course, I'd watch that again and again.

The rest of the afternoon was devoted to planning the short trip to Cambridge. After a while, I excused myself to get a glass of milk.

I walked down the hall toward the kitchen, then heard a shout from the family room. Backtracking, I found the door open just wide enough to reveal Shiloh standing against a wall, arms folded tightly over his chest, head down. He cut a lonely figure, like something heavy was weighing on his mind. I almost knocked, but then I saw his father step close, and a chill ran down my spine.

"I refuse to allow this," his father growled. "You will not withdraw from this competition just to give that pitiful poor girl a chance."

"Her name is Anela," Shiloh said quietly. "It's not Anna or 'that poor girl.'"

"I don't care what her name is."

This was a private moment between father and son that I had no business eavesdropping on. But something anchored me to the spot. Even if this conversation had nothing to do with me, it had everything to do with me.

A familiar fear clawed at my insides. The fear I'd felt when Mom and Dad were going at each other, not caring what they said or who was listening. I did my best to block that past from seeping back in, but the situation wasn't helping.

"I didn't get where I am by standing back for anyone else, and neither will you," Mr. Parker said. "Do you read me? I don't care if you don't want the scholarship, Shiloh. I only care that you win. What you do reflects on this family."

I didn't know what to think of Shiloh wanting to pull out of the competition to give me a better chance. On the one hand, I was astonished that he cared so much. On the other hand, I couldn't help but feel that Shiloh underestimated my ability to win the essay competition without his help.

Shiloh avoided looking at his father, who appeared ready to explode. The veins in Mr. Parker's neck throbbed with rage. "Look at me! Tell me you understand."

When Shiloh's gaze remained firmly averted, his father did the unimaginable. He hit Shiloh so hard that his son staggered sideways. The impact sent a shiver through me. I wanted to go in there and tear that man apart for hurting Shiloh. But I put my thoughts in single file to get hold of my feelings and stood back, my fingernails biting into the palms of my hands.

There was a long, scary silence as Shiloh's father stewed and continued to stare down his son. "You don't think of anyone but yourself," he hissed. "Your last name is Parker. Don't you forget that for one second. You will not allow that girl to ruin your life. You'll go out and win this thing."

"She is not 'that girl,'" Shiloh said, finally meeting his father's glare. "Her name is Anela Lee. And I love her."

Tears sprang to my eyes. *"And I love her."* I wanted to wrap that sentence up and stow it away in my heart for eternity.

"And you're right," Shiloh said. "I shouldn't withdraw from the competition. Because Anela can win this all by herself." And with that, my roiling emotions were reconciled.

Mr. Parker was speechless at Shiloh's refusal to back down. He stormed for the door, and I ducked into the next room, holding my breath. When I was sure he was gone, I went in to see Shiloh. He didn't seem surprised to see me but wiped his tears away. I moved close and wrapped him in my arms, wanting only for him to feel love and warmth. After a while, the tension left him. I stood back and looked at his cheek, where an ugly bruise was forming.

"Wait here. I'll get some ice," I said.

"Thank you," Shiloh replied. "Anela?"

"Yeah?"

"I meant what I said."

I snagged an ice pack from the kitchen, keeping an eye out for Mr. Parker the whole time. When I got back to Shiloh, I went into nurse mode. Jake had taught me some basic first aid stuff, like putting ice on a contusion, pouring cold water on a minor burn, cleaning cuts with mild soap and running water. I sat on the couch, and Shiloh rested his head on my lap while I held the ice pack to his cheek. We talked about everything. He told me about the book he was writing. I told him about Senator Strasberg finding her sister. And we made a pact: the essay competition would never come between us.

"I mean, there are three other finalists," I said. "Any one of them could win."

Shiloh laughed. "Exactly."

"I have to get back to Tamara," I said reluctantly. "I'm already behind on the schoolwork with her."

"I'm sure one day won't make a difference," Shiloh said. "I can help her catch up."

"You'll be my hero if you can help her with algebra," I said. "Then I can spend more time with her on other subjects. I hate algebra."

He smirked. "I mean, if I can be your hero . . . But really, no problem. I love algebra."

I scrutinized his cheek. At least the swelling had gone down a bit.

"What are you going to tell your mom?" I asked.

"The truth," he said. "That he's a bully. That he hit me because for once I stood up to him."

"Thank you for defending me," I said. "You could have made it easier on yourself, but you chose the hard way. And I want you to know I appreciate it."

"I acted like a dork that night, after our date," he said. "That was so wrong on every level."

"To be honest, I kinda forgave you when I found that white rosebud at my locker." My phone dinged with a text—Mom, asking what I wanted for dinner. Food was the last thing on my mind, but she was making up for lost time, so I texted back: "You've been working too hard. How about I bring you pizza? I really want to."

"Okay, baby. Bring me pizza. No onions, no peppers, and extra cheese plse." She sent a ton of smiley faces and hearts. I had to smile; she was getting the hang of this mom/daughter text thing.

Shiloh rose from the couch and held out a hand. When he helped me up, we were suddenly standing very close. The butterflies in my stomach went crazy. Shiloh nudged a rebellious curl of hair from my cheek and kissed me gently.

"One more thing," he said as we pulled apart. "I'd love it if you would join the newspaper's editorial team. I need a regular columnist to write about social topics kids can relate to. You know, the things nobody wants to talk about out loud."

My mind was immediately spinning with ideas. "Sure. Thanks. I'll start working on some ideas tonight and text them to you."

He grinned. "You mean this is all I had to do to get your number? Well then, welcome to the team."

On my way to Tamara's room, I nearly crashed into Shiloh's father going around a corner. There was no squeezing past him, and pride wouldn't let me look anywhere but right into his eyes. I tried to hear Jake's voice to help me through the encounter, but there was nothing. Maybe he was silent because he'd already taught me enough.

"Hi, Mr. Parker," I said.

I expected him to be gruff and brush past me, but he didn't. It was almost like he was waiting for me to speak my mind.

"You know," I said, "I think you're a good man who's petrified his son will make the wrong choices in life. But let me tell you something. The Shiloh I know is a kind, very smart, and gentle soul who's scared of his father. What's really happening is that you're pushing him away. And one day he's going to leave, and you'll never see him again.

"I saw you hit him. I never thought I would have to tell a grown man to get help with anger management, and I don't know what happened in your life to make you like this, but seriously, you're making your family miserable. Worse than that is you're using me as an excuse to act out. I don't care what you think of me, but I'm almost sure I'm not the problem here. If I were you, I'd apologize to Shiloh and make peace. You have one son, so why don't you just love him and acknowledge that you've raised a pretty spectacular boy? And if you could let me past, I'd appreciate it."

He took his time stepping aside. I felt his stare burning my back, but I didn't look around until I reached Tamara's room. Then I went in and shut the door behind me.

"So, I just got a text from Shiloh," Tamara said. "Apparently he's helping me with algebra now?" Then she smiled. "I'm almost sure there's something you have to tell me. Take a seat, Miss Lee, and fill me in on what happened between you and my brother."

So I did, mostly. Later that night, I got a text from Shiloh.

"SO MY DAD HAD A TALK WITH ME TONIGHT. HE APOLOGIZED AND PROMISED TO DO BETTER. AND GET THIS, HE SAID HE DIDN'T CARE IF I WON, BECAUSE AS LONG AS I HAVE YOU IN MY CORNER, I'M ALREADY A WINNER. I'M STILL TRYING TO PICK MY JAW UP FROM THE FLOOR."

I smiled widely. I didn't share what I'd said to Mr. Parker with either of them, but I was glad things turned out well.

• • •

The closer we got to the big day, the more nervous I got, despite trying to appear pretty relaxed about the whole deal. The night before, I sat in my room and reviewed the section I planned to read aloud, wondering if it was the right passage and whether I could pull it off.

Mom knocked on the door.

"Come in."

She sat on my bed and handed me a cup of tea. "It's chamomile," she said. "Should help you sleep better."

"Thanks. I'm so nervous about reading this in front of people."

Mom's gaze was so proud that I wanted to cry. "You shouldn't be. You're going to be great. And even if you stumble, you pick yourself right up and go on."

I jumped off the bed, grabbed Mom's hand, and dragged her into Jake's room.

"I have a new quote to paint," I said. "Come."

Mom sat on Jake's bed and watched as I painted my new quote on an empty spot above Jake's desk:

"EVEN IF YOU STUMBLE, YOU PICK YOURSELF RIGHT UP AND GO ON."
SOPHIA LEE

• • •

Mom woke me before dawn. "Time to get ready." She told me Isabel had called to say we would all meet up at Starbucks.

I leaped out of bed, ready to take on the day. When Mom came out of her bedroom, all made up and dressed to the nines, I gasped.

"Wow! Look at you. You look beautiful!" I contemplated what kind of life Mom might have led if she hadn't settled for this one. She was a gorgeous woman. My heart expanded with love and pride.

By the time the Uber dropped us off at Starbucks, the adrenaline had worn off a bit, and the old anxiety crept back in. We met the

Parkers inside. I was happy to see color in Tamara's cheeks again. Shiloh greeted me with a casual kiss on the cheek. He must have put makeup over the bruise.

"How are the other finalists supposed to compete with this?" he whispered. "Beauty and brains."

My skin tingled with happiness. "Right back at you."

"Hey, A," someone called from behind me.

"Troy!" I said, surprised. "I had no idea you were coming."

"Wouldn't miss it for anything, A," Troy replied. "Besides, they needed someone to film it live because the entire school is watching." He took a seat by Tamara, who was beaming.

Mr. Parker took charge of ordering coffee. I was nervous about coming face-to-face with him again, but he gave me a secret wink when he handed me my coffee and pastry. I knew then everything would be cool. Speaking of which, he'd rented a limousine to take us all to Cambridge in style, even though it was just a few miles away.

The sun was rising when Shiloh and I climbed into the limo. Everyone else was still in Starbucks. Shiloh held my hand, and we looked through the window cheek to cheek.

"That sunrise is the most magical thing I've ever seen," I said.

"Maybe you should get used to the limo view," Shiloh told me. "There are big things in your future."

"If I win," I said. "If not, it's back to square one, and I try something else."

"You have at least as good a shot as I do," Shiloh said. And he meant it.

The Starbucks door opened, and our families came out. Mr. Parker's gaze met mine for a moment, and he nodded. I nodded back. Everyone got in except Troy, who took his own car. He and Tamara stood awfully close before they parted ways.

CHAPTER 25

Soon enough, we arrived on the Harvard campus for the final. It was strange to think the place had been so close all along. I soaked up the feeling of being there and thought of the many ways Jake had helped with the journey. He'd pushed me to use my mind and not be confined by our broken family circle. He watched over me as I explored the world and always encouraged me to reach for the sky. Now here I was, surrounded by people I loved, who loved me back. Mom stood next to me and held my hand. We both felt the power of that moment.

"Nothing stands in your way anymore, baby," she whispered. "And I'll be right here with you, all the way."

When we reached the auditorium, Shiloh and I were rushed backstage to meet the other finalists and the judges. And much as I tried to stay calm, my nerves grew frayed.

"How are you not nervous?" I asked Shiloh.

He charmed me with a smile. "It's like my dad said: with you by my side, I'm already a winner."

Shiloh and I and the other finalists were ushered into a room showing a live feed of the stage. I was the only girl in there. I couldn't be happier to have Shiloh by my side. Our guide told us that our names would be called one by one, at which point we'd be taken to the lectern on the stage. We'd read from our essays and then sit in the front row.

Shiloh and I were up against some brilliant and confident kids. I pushed back at my self-doubt as the other three finalists delivered flawless readings. Soon, Shiloh and I were the only ones left. Talk about pressure.

When my name was finally called and Shiloh wished me luck, I was sure my legs would give out before I reached the microphone. I made it, though, and closed my eyes for a moment, praying for inner calm. When I opened my eyes again, the same massive audience stared back.

Yet I felt the fear leave me. I had nothing to be nervous about. Those closest to me were here for me, with no judgment or expectation. They wanted me to be happy and do my best.

There was only one face absent from the crowd.

"I'm dedicating my essay to the memory of my brother, Jake," I said, my voice soft but finding its strength. I didn't need notes to read my passage. I knew it by heart.

"This excerpt is from my essay on trauma:

"Your past is not the same as your future unless you live in that past. Two people can endure the same trauma and experience radically different outcomes. One retreats into herself, relives the trauma every day in her head, and never trusts anyone again. She may even turn to drugs, or worse. Another uses the same situation to fuel anger, or compassion, or maybe both. She decides she'll never be a victim again and remakes herself to be stronger, more aware. Maybe she decides to help others in her situation to do the same. She moves on and never looks back.

"One of these women is convinced that because this terrible thing happened, she'll never be the same. She'll always be less than she was before. The other is convinced she'll never be the same either—because she'll be stronger. They're both right. Because trauma is not what makes or unmakes us. The meaning we draw from it and what we do about it does. 'This means my life is ruined, and I'll always be picking up the pieces' vs. 'This means that will never happen again because I'm stronger now, mentally, physically, spiritually. And if I can get past something like that, I can handle anything life throws at me.'

"Søren Kierkegaard said, 'Life can only be understood backwards; but it must be lived forwards.' He also said, 'Our life always expresses the result of our dominant thoughts.' Again, right on both counts. If all you ever do is think about some awful thing you experienced, that thing will consume you, heart and soul. If, instead, you use that awful thing to push you into becoming fitter, wiser, more alert, it can empower you.

"But here's a twist. It's not only about you or me, how we view ourselves singularly. What matters most is *us*, how we see others through the lens of our suffering, and the subsequent strength we find, corporately, to remember that our view of who we are in the world is influenced by those who help us in our darkest times, those who provide us with opportunities—and, further down the road, how we give back."

I took a few seconds to find the faces I knew: everyone who'd helped me get there. Mom, who was trying not to cry. Miss DeGracia, who smiled up at me with Mr. Lanfelt seated next to her. He looked like a different man. Nastasia Strasberg was there too, with her sister, Hien, beside her. Mayumi, whose gaze was reassuring and full of pride. There was Tamara, and her parents. Even Monique was there, all blinged out at the end of a row. She gave me a little wave with her rhinestone-encrusted phone. And I spotted Troy behind a camera. In some sense, Malala, Anne, Huss, Mils, Blythe, Dutch, Fitz, Ellen, Margaret, Indira, and Benazir were with me too.

"Elisabeth Elliot said, 'Our vision is so limited we can hardly imagine a love that does not show itself in protection from suffering.... A lot of hammering and chiseling and purifying by fire will have to go into the process.' That's true. But whether those fires consume us or forge us into something stronger is up to us."

When I finished, a moment of rapt silence preceded thundering applause. It took a second for me to realize they were applauding me and the words I'd written. I smiled and left the stage to take my seat beside the other three finalists.

Shiloh's name was called next. He strode toward the mic in his confident, charming way, and my heart went into overdrive. As I listened to him speak passionately about what we were doing to the planet, I hoped he'd win. This was his last chance to enter the competition. I still had next year.

When Shiloh finished reading, his gaze found mine, and he winked. He looked like a completely different Shiloh than the one from a month ago. He seemed at peace with himself and the world, freed from the baggage of his father's wrath. After the applause died down, he sat beside me. I touched his arm and whispered, "You make it seem so easy. How do you do it?"

"Listen to who's talking," he replied. "You spoke like a pro. And, might I add, looked good doing it. The camera loves you—I'll tell you that."

I was still blushing at the compliment when a photographer stepped in front of us to take pictures of the finalists. Then he turned his attention to me.

"Can I get a picture of you alone, please?" he asked.

I was confused. "Why?"

"You have to ask? Even if you don't win, my guess is you'll be the face of this competition for years to come."

"Even if she didn't win?" Shiloh asked with a smirk. "Bro, of course she won."

The other three finalists looked at each other; I thought I saw them roll their eyes.

Up on the stage, the head judge stepped to the podium, adjusted the mic, and cleared his throat to get everyone's attention. "Good morning . . . Hello . . . Well, sorry to say there's been a little hiccup, and we'll have a short delay before announcing the winner. We appreciate your patience."

A murmur rose in the auditorium, everyone wondering what the delay could be. The judge glanced our way and then hurried backstage. He looked a little worried. One of the finalists, a boy my age, leaned in and whispered conspiratorially, "Maybe one of us is getting kicked out. Three years ago, a finalist got disqualified because they discovered that two of his paragraphs were plagiarized."

"Why did they only figure that out after he was a finalist?" Shiloh asked.

"He read the plagiarized bits to the audience," the boy said. "Someone recognized it and told the judges."

Before we could speculate further, the judge was back at the podium. He appeared less worried and mustered a smile. "What's about to happen has never happened before. You could say it's history in the making. We have two winners this year. Two young people who delivered remarkable essays.

"After some discussion, the judges have decided to drop the formalities and award both winners a cash prize and a full scholarship to a local college. Provided their GPAs are 4.0 or above, of course, and they meet all requirements, including standardized test scores. In addition, a recommendation will be offered to the Harvard admissions committee should the winner decide to pursue that opportunity where other distinctions are likely to be required."

The audience cheered. I smiled, but my stomach was in a tight knot. Shiloh and I exchanged looks. We both knew how much was on the line. We wanted different things from this competition. Shiloh wanted the satisfaction of winning. I wanted the scholarship—and the cash prize was pretty cool, too.

"You know it's not the end of the world if neither of us gets it, right?" Shiloh whispered. I nodded, but inside I fought against that notion. It might not be the end of the world because I could enter again next year, but how great would it be to lock in the scholarship and not have to worry about it? Earning a scholarship because of the work I'd put in would mean everything to me.

I glanced back at Mom. She had her eyes closed and her hands folded in her lap. I knew she was praying. The judge studied the paper in his hand, blissfully unaware of the tension he was creating. Or maybe it was deliberate.

He cleared his throat. "The first winner is Shiloh Parker for his essay on climate change. Please come up here, Shiloh."

Applause reverberated through the auditorium. Shiloh hesitated, turning to me. I kissed him on the cheek, tears of joy in my eyes. "They're waiting for you. Go, Shiloh!"

Shiloh moved reluctantly up the steps, shook the judge's hand, and accepted his winner's certificate and cashier's check. He kept looking at me like he wanted to apologize for winning. I smiled, genuinely happy for him.

The judge again analyzed the paper in his hand as if the secrets of the cosmos were written there. "Okay, so we are on to the next winn—"

Someone yelled out, "ANELA!" before he could finish. It sounded suspiciously like Monique. Then someone else yelled my name, and soon a chorus was chanting. The other three finalists definitely rolled their eyes this time. The wall damming my emotions started to crack, and my nails bit into my palms.

The judge grinned. "Well, what do you know? The other winner is indeed Anela Lee!"

The chant gave way to wild applause, whistles, and yelling. I stared at Mom. She didn't try to hold the tears back. I hurried up to the stage, where Shiloh embraced me. Even the judge seemed swept up in the moment. He leaned into the mic. "Well, there you have it: a match made in academic heaven. Congratulations to you both."

• • •

Sometime during the afternoon reception, Shiloh grabbed my hand. We left the crowd and went outside.

"What do you say we do our own tour of Harvard?" Shiloh said. "Explore the grounds, get lost, and find our way again?"

I nodded, smiling until my face hurt. "I'd love that! I can't believe Harvard is really possible."

As we walked the pathways thousands of students had trod over the centuries, I felt at home. I knew I belonged here. But there was more for me to do. Of course, Shiloh was almost a given.

"It's a pity you'll be a year ahead of me," I said. "But we'll make it work."

"You ever heard of a gap year?" Shiloh asked. "I have it all worked out. I take a year off and write the great American novel while patiently waiting for you to finish high school. You're all set for a local college. Work toward getting into Harvard, whatever it takes. Then we'll go together."

"How would your dad feel about that?"

Shiloh grinned. "He's the one who suggested it."

The sun was setting as the limo took us back over the Charles River to Boston. Shiloh and I stared through the window, cheek to cheek once again. I pressed the locket with Jake's picture close to my heart.

"Better get used to this Harvard-to-Boston view, Shi," I said. "We might be seeing a lot of it."

The End

REFLECTIVE QUESTIONS

1. What is your favorite part of Anela's experiences?

2. What character in the story do you identify with the most?

3. Describe what you believe to be the turning point in the story. Why did you choose that?

4. If you were Anela, is there anything you would do differently?

5. Who helped Anela most: Jake, Miss DeGracia, Senator Strasberg, or Shilo? Why?

6. Jake and Anela love quotes. Is there a quote from the story that you appreciated?

7. If you knew someone like Anela, how would you treat her?

8. Who challenged you most to look at your life differently?

9. How does Anela's story relate to you?

10. What do you think about Anela's idea for her "club"?

11. If you had a "club," who would be in it?

12. In what ways might Anela and Tamara's friendship relate to your friendships?

ACKNOWLEDGMENTS

I first imagined Anela and her family while walking the neighborhoods of Brookline, Massachusetts. That led to conversations with family and friends in such places as a taqueria in Harvard Square, along MIT's Main Street, an apartment at Coolidge Corner, dining rooms in Honolulu, Los Angeles, and Washington DC, a university north of Chicago, and the Tom Quad of Christ Church, Oxford.

Deepest gratitude to those who nurtured the dream of *Anela*—my conversation partners, supporters, and literary team: Dr. Micah Maetani, Cathy Suehisa, Luke Yamashiro, Hugh Yamashiro, Dr. Allie Yamashiro, Jamie Yamashiro, Dr. Hugh Dunn, Dr. Rebecca Gibbs, Jimmy and Diana Yamada, Guy Shindo, Dr. Kerry Ishihara, Edward Shiroma, Dr. Scott Tan, Jamie Nelson, David Keawe Holt, John Foy, Charlie Chimento, Suzanne Maurer, Lani Kaaa, Sam and Nancy Webb, Joy Miyazawa, Griffin Frank, Marin Frank, Kimberly Frank, Jonathan Steeper, Norman Nakanishi, Dr. George Nagato, Dr. Dan Chun, Mike Kai, Camille Omo, Dr. Donald and Mary Guthrie, Dr. Seth Nelson, Anthony Wainana Njuguna, Stacy Lung, Dr. Doug Bond, Dr. Gary Scott Smith, Todd Rankin, Dr. Andrew Chaney, Keith Chinen, David and Alice Yamashiro, David and Ululani Yamashiro, Iolani Yamashiro-Rahimi, Hani Rahimi, Dr. Ethan and Shannon Small, Timothy Lyons, Kim Nguyen, Ronnie Glenn, Dr. Yared and Alana Gurmu, Ed and Mae Jung, Dr. Stephen Mansfield, Sam Huggard, Dr. Todd Hall, Dr. Livia Blackburne, Ross Browne, John Robert Marlow, Jacqueline Sinclair, Karinya Funsett-Topping, J. Mark Ramseyer, Victoria Strauss, Thecla Ree, Kevin Mayew, Jean Yamashiro, Tasha Babers, John Köehler, Hannah Woodlan, Christine Kettner, Joe Coccaro, and Lauren Sheldon.

Dominus Illuminatio Mea

REFERENCES

CHAPTER 4

"We ask ourselves, Who am I": This quote is often attributed to Nelson Mandela but was first written by Marianne Williamson in her best-selling self-help book *A Return to Love* (1992).

Constance Grady, "Why Marianne Williamson's most famous passage keeps getting cited as a Nelson Mandela quote: The most well-known passage Marianne Willamson wrote has some disconcerting implications," *Vox*, July 30, 2019, https://www.vox.com/culture/2019/7/30/20699833/marianne-williamson-our-deepest-fear-nelson-mandela-return-to-love.

"Once I had asked God": Malala Yousafzai and Christina Lamb, *I Am Malala: The Girl Who Stood Up for Education and Was Shot by the Taliban* (New York: Little, Brown and Company, 2013), 264.

CHAPTER 8

"Twenty years from now": This quote from H. Jackson Brown's *P.S. I Love You* (1990) is attributed to his mother, Sarah Frances Brown.

Matt Seybold, "The Apocryphal Twain: 'The Things You Didn't Do," *Center for Mark Twain Studies*, June 28, 2019, https://marktwainstudies.com/the-apocryphal-twain-the-things-you-didnt-do/.

CHAPTER 11

Let's call him Huss: "Huss" is the abbreviated version for Barack

Hussein Obama. "Rack" is used to refer to President Obama's father, Barack Hussein Obama, Sr. The author has taken the liberty to use these abbreviations to tell the story of Anela.

His mother's name was Stanley: Barack Obama, *Dreams from My Father: A Story of Race and Inheritance* (New York: Crown Publishers, 2004), 5.

"After a week of seeing my father": Obama, *Dreams*, 63.

Huss moved to Indonesia: Obama, *Dreams*, 37–38.

One day, a man with no nose: Obama, *Dreams*, 37.

That's twelve-year-old Mils: "Mils" is the abbreviated version the author uses to refer to Richard Milhous Nixon.

He was such a talented piano player: Jonathan Aitken, *Nixon: A Life* (London: Weidenfeld and Nicolson, 1993), 24.

Mils's family were Quakers: Stephen E. Ambrose, *Nixon, Volume 1: The Education of a Politician 1913–1962* (New York: Simon and Schuster, 1988), 30.

Mils loved his little brother: Conrad Black, *Richard Milhous Nixon: The Invincible Quest* (London: Quercus, 2007), 16. See Roger Morris, *Richard Milhous Nixon: The Rise of an American Politician* (New York: Holt, 1989), 84.

He prayed for Arthur: Aitken, *Nixon*, 26.

Mils sank into a "deep, impenetrable silence": Black, *Invincible Quest*, 16; Morris, *American Politician*, 84.

CHAPTER 16

I felt my cheeks burn: Evan Andrews, "Who was the First Woman to Run for President? Victoria Woodhull ran for highest office nearly 50 years before women gained the right to vote," *History*, March 4, 2020, https://www.history.com/news/who-was-the-first-woman-to-run-for-president.

But okay . . . Frederick Douglas: Andrews, "Who was the First Woman."

CHAPTER 20

So there was this girl who was sixteen: Ellen Johnson Sirleaf, *This Child Will Be Great: Memoir of a Remarkable Life by Africa's First Woman President* (New York: HarperCollins, 2009), 23.

He became paralyzed before her eyes: Helene Cooper, *Madame President: The Extraordinary Journey of Ellen Johnson Sirleaf* (New York: Simon & Schuster, 2017), 7.

Also as a teen: Sirleaf, *This Child Will Be Great*, 7.

Then there was Margaret Thatcher: John Campbell, *Margaret Thatcher, Volume One: The Grocer's Daughter* (London: Jonathan Cape), 38.

Okay, then there was the six-year-old girl: Pupul Jayakar, *Indira Gandhi: A Biography* (New Delhi: Viking, 1992), 21.

She didn't see her father: Jayakar, *Indira*, 21.

Her aunt called her "ugly and stupid": Jayakar, Indira, 44–45.

Okay, another girl was fifteen: Benazir Bhutto, *Daughter of the East: An Autobiography* (London: Simon & Schuster, 2007), 44.

Her father told her not to look: Bhutto, *Daughter*, 44.

CHAPTER 22

Let's call him by his birth name, Blythe: "Blythe" is the name the author uses for William Jefferson Clinton III. His birth name was William Jefferson Blythe III. His father, William Jefferson Blythe, Jr., died three months before he was born.

At three, he was already living with his grandparents: Bill Clinton, *My Life* (New York: Vintage Books, 2004), 8.

"His memory infused me": Clinton, *My Life*, 7.

"The knowledge that I, too": Clinton, *My Life*, 7.

He was bullied by others: Clinton, *My Life*, 12.

When Blythe approached the doorway: Clinton, *My Life*, 19–20.

When Blythe was fourteen: Clinton, *My Life*, 45.

Another time, Roger bent Blythe's mother over: Nigel Hamilton, *Bill Clinton: An American Journey: Great Expectations* (New York: Random House, 2003), 115–116. Hamilton cites: Virginia Kelley and James Morgan, *Leading with My Heart* (New York: Simon & Schuster, 1994), 160–161.

Later in life, Blythe acknowledged: Clinton, *My Life*, 15.

CHAPTER 23

When Dutch was young: "Dutch" was the nickname given to Ronald Wilson Reagan by his father, Jack, who said that he looked like a "fat little Dutchman."

His father was a shoe salesman: Garry Wills, *Reagan's America: Innocents at Home* (Garden City, NY: Doubleday & Company, Inc., 1987), 15.

Dutch said she encouraged him: Anne Edwards, *Early Reagan* (New York: Morrow, 1987), 60.

But there was a dark side to Dutch's family: Edwards, *Early Reagan*, 57.

One cold winter's night: Ronald Reagan, *An American Life* (New York: Simon & Schuster, 2011), 33.

But Nelle taught him: Reagan, *American Life*, 20–21.

There once was a boy . . . Let's call him Fitz: "Fitz" is the abbreviated middle name of John Fitzgerald Kennedy. His mother's name full name was Rose Elizabeth Fitzgerald Kennedy. The author derived "Beth" from Elizabeth. His father's full name was Joseph Patrick Kennedy, Sr. The author uses the name "Patrick" in telling the story of Anela.

One day, Beth announced she was going: Nigel Hamilton, *JFK: Reckless Youth* (New York: Random House, 1992), 47.

Their mom never kissed them: Hamilton, *Reckless Youth*, 48.

Fitz told a friend that despite his sadness: Peter J. Ling, *John F. Kennedy* (New York: Routledge, 2013), 9.

Fitz suffered a lot of illnesses: Rose Kennedy, *Times to Remember* (Garden City, NY: Doubleday & Company, 1974), 84; Thomas C. Reeves, *A Question of Character: A Life of John F. Kennedy* (New York: Maxwell Macmillan International, 1991), 39. Reeves cites: Joan Blair and Clay Blair, Jr., *The Search for JFK* (New York: Berkley Publishing Corporation, 1976), 15–16. See also Herbert S. Parmet, *Jack: The Struggles of John F. Kennedy* (New York: Dial Press, 1980), 21; Robert Dallek, *An Unfinished Life: John F. Kennedy, 1917–1963* (Boston: Little, Brown, and Co., 2003), 34; Parmet, *Struggles*, 17; Geoffrey Perret, *Jack: A Life Like No Other* (New York: Random House, 2001), 37; Blair and Blair, Jr., *Search for JFK*, 24; Parmet, *Struggles*, 15. See Joan Meyers, ed., *John Fitzgerald Kennedy: As We Remember Him* (New York: Atheneum, 1965), vi.

AUTHOR

As a teen, D. K. Yamashiro survived falling four hundred feet from a ridge in Hawaii, suffering severe brain injuries. Years of recovery involved a camel ride at the Pyramids of Giza, swimming in the Mediterranean Sea, hiking up Masada, sledding down the Great Wall of China, exploring underground caves in the Black Hills, and speaking to crowds in East Africa and Brazilian favelas. A master's at Harvard and summer studies at Oxford preceded a PhD with research on childhood traumas of American presidents. Yamashiro is an affiliate at MIT.

www.ingramcontent.com/pod-product-compliance
Lightning Source LLC
LaVergne TN
LVHW041935070526
838199LV00051BA/2798